Close To Sleigh Bells

A Westen Series Christmas Novel

Suzanne Ferrell

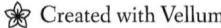

Acknowledgments

The Ferrell team always deserves a big thank you!

I'd like to thank my cover artist, Lyndsey Lewellen of LLewellen Designs. Your covers are making the fictional town of Westen come alive!

Thank you Alison Beach for editing this story for me. Thanks for fixing all my comma issues, and giving Harriett only two t's and not three!

Dear Reader

Thank you so much for trying my Indie published book. I understand that there are many options for you to spend your money on and am honored that you chose one of my books. For that reason my team and I strive to put out the best product we can from the awesome cover design through the entire editing and formatting process. For my part, I hope to deliver an entertaining story that keeps you wondering what's going to happen next.

If at the end of this book you find you simply loved the story and characters, please consider giving it a positive <u>rating or review</u>. In this brave new book world, the only way for a good story to find its way into the hands of other readers is if the people who loved it let others know about it. We authors appreciate any little bit of help you can give us.

If, when you reach the end of this story, you think, "Wow, I'd love to know what's next in Suzanne's world of characters," then consider joining my <u>newsletter mailing list</u>. I only send out newsletters a few times a year, plus extra ones in anticipation of any new releases, so it won't be flooding your inbox on a weekly basis, but will keep you abreast on any changes I may have coming.

Also, I love to hear from readers. If you have any questions or comments, or just want to say "hi", please feel free to visit my webpage for some extra tidbits or check out my Pinterest boards. You can connect with me via Facebook, Twitter or through my email: suzanne@suzanneferrell.com

One new place to contact me is through my REAM subscription service. You can check it out here: REAM

Now the important part: Here's Noel and Monty's story. I hope you will love them as much as I did while writing **Close To Sleigh Bells.**

Suzanne

Chapter One

"Dad, I'm going to be late," Noel Fisher's thirteen year-old daughter Callie whined from the backdoor.

For the first time since the school year began three months ago, she was dressed, had eaten her breakfast and was actually ready to leave for school ten minutes before they needed to depart. His radar went off. Something was up.

"We have plenty of time, Callie."

Slowly, he finished his coffee and rinsed out the mug before setting it in the dishwasher with the rest of the morning dishes. He should have known she had something on her agenda today when she emptied and loaded the dishwasher without her usual prodding last night. It was a toss-up between chores and home-work as to which one got the most complaints.

"So, why are you in such a hurry to get to school today?" he asked as he grabbed his denim jacket and keys from the hooks by the back door where she was holding the screen open for him. He barely had time to catch it as she let go and dashed down the steps and to the passenger side of his truck.

"There's going to be a horse at school," she said once they were both buckled into their seatbelts.

That explains it. While he was on an overseas assignment this summer, Callie not only turned into a teenager, but developed a love of all things equestrian. So much so, that his brother Nick, whom she'd been living with while he was out of town, had suggested they go in halves to buy her a horse of her own. If that was the only cost, he'd happily agree. Except he had nowhere to keep a horse in the town of Westen, unless he wanted to sell his house and buy some farmland.

"Why are they having a horse at school today?" he asked as he pulled out of the driveway, taking a second to return the wave to Mr. Gordon out walking his two large white Pyrenees dogs.

"Aunt Holly says it's a career day event."

Holly, his brother Nick's wife, was the drama and music teacher for the new middle school and one of the elementary schools in town.

"What kind of career has to do with horses?"

"I don't know, Daddy," Callie said with that new exasperated tone she used when asked a question she didn't know the answer to but was irritated it was asked of her at all. "I just want to see them."

Again, his warning system sounded, as he pulled up to the entrance to the school at the same time a horse trailer was driving into the side parking lot. Callie already had her seatbelt off before he'd even stopped the car. He grabbed her arm. "Wait."

"Why? Daddy, the horse is right there!"

"I see that. I think I'd like to see the horse too. So, let me park and we'll walk over."

She heaved a heavy sigh—something new she'd started since

stepping into her teens—but stayed put in the car. He hid his grin. She thought her actions showed her exasperation and would irritate him into giving into her demands. It might if he was a different person. Instead, it amused him. At some point she'd outgrow the rather childish display. In the meantime, he'd take advantage to see how often he could elicit the response from her until she grew tired of losing the battles. He was *that* kind of parent. The one who was in charge.

Once they were parked, she hopped out, slung her backpack on her shoulders, but waited to walk with him over to the trailer, where a woman was leading a brown horse with a black mane from the horse trailer.

"That must be Monty," Callie said, almost hopping up and down with joy like she did when she was a toddler excited by a new experience.

"Who's Monty?" he asked looking around for a man.

"She is!" Callie pointed to the woman walking the horse over to a green spot near a tree. "Aunt Holly says she owns the Gentle Creek Ranch. She's who's going to talk to us about the horses."

Monty. Unusual name for a woman. As they neared, she turned their way. He almost stopped in his tracks. She was lovely. Tallish for a woman, maybe five-foot seven, willowy thin, dark auburn hair pulled back in a braid, startling blue eyes and just a dusting of freckles over her nose and cheeks. Her tanned skin spoke of hours working outdoors. But it was her smile that really hit him hard.

"You must be Holly's niece and brother-in-law?" she asked.

Startled that she knew who they were, he did stop and looked at her curiously. "We are. I'm Nick Fisher and this is my daughter Callie. How did you know?"

"Holly and I have been friends for several months now. You

3

do look a lot like your brother," she said, extending her hand. "I'm Montgomery Taylor. Monty to friends."

He shook her hand. Even though her slender hands were dwarfed by his, he liked the feel of the calluses on her palm and the strength of her grip. This wasn't some debutant who just rode horses. If she owned a horse farm, she certainly worked hard on it. "Glad to meet you. Callie tells me you and your horse are here for some sort of career day event?"

"What's his name?" Callie asked swaying a little on her feet, trying to contain her excitement.

"*Her* name is Sugarplum," Monty said, stepping to the side of the mare's head, her hand firmly holding the reins. "Would you like to pet her?"

"Can I?" Callie asked. She sounded like a child again instead of a young lady on the steps of womanhood.

"Of course. She loves to have her coat stroked. You can start with her forehead."

Callie stepped over and tentatively touched the horse's nose, then stroked her hand down the center. The horse seemed to watch her from one eye and Noel held his breath slightly, prepared to pull Callie away if the horse tried to bite at her. But the beast that was several inches taller than his daughter seemed to enjoy her touch even slightly leaning her head into Callie's hand.

"She likes me!" Callie said petting Sugarplum more confidently.

Monty laughed. It wasn't a young girl's giggle or a faked humorless indulgent sound. No. It was warm and welcoming like a finely aged bourbon that warms a man from the inside out.

"Of course, she does. You're happy to see her and she spends a lot of her time with kids and teens. She's a very gentle, sensitive lady."

"You have kids then?" Noel asked.

"No. I've never had any of my own."

Before he could ask further, his sister-in-law approached, a distinct waddle in her gait. In a month's time, her second child, a girl this time, was due.

"Monty! You made it," Holly said, giving the other woman one of those hugs women seemed to always give friends, before hugging Callie and then him. "I see you've met my family."

"I have," Monty said. "I was just letting Sugarplum stretch her legs and nibble in the grass a bit before we head..." She paused a moment, looking around. "Where exactly do you want me to set up my things?"

"Oh, we've got you out on the football practice field, if you want to follow me," Holly said, turning to head to the back of the school.

The school buses had arrived by the time they got to the back of the building, and they were almost swarmed by the younger teens climbing off them. Nick immediately moved between the kids and the horse.

"Hold on kids!" he said in his deepest I'm-in-charge-and-you're-not voice and holding his arms out wide. Most of the crowd stopped, except for few boys, including twin red-heads intent on breaching the distance to the horse, who surprisingly hadn't spooked at the wave of humanity and noise headed her way. Monty seemed just as non-plussed.

"Ben and Brian, could you go get the two saddles out of the back of my truck for me?" she asked.

"Sure thing, Monty," the twins said in unison and took a right turn.

Out of nowhere a large body came in behind the other kids. "Y'all need to get to your homerooms," Deputy Cleetus Junkins announced. As if on cue, the first bell for school sounded. "You can see Miss Taylor and her horse during the career day fair."

The kids all moaned, but they turned and started moving in the direction of the school.

"That includes you, Callie," Noel said and held his breath wondering if she was going to give him an argument.

Instead, she patted the mare once more and smiled at her owner. "Thanks for letting me pet Sugarplum."

"You're more than welcome, Callie. I'll look for you during your social studies period."

Callie gave Noel a kiss on the cheek and whispered, "Thanks, Daddy," before she jogged to the school, meeting up with her friend Rowan waited for her.

Noel looked around, knowing he needed to get on to the worksite and get his day started, but wanted to find out more about Monty and what kind of career talk she was giving the kids.

"We got the saddles, Monty," Ben Lewis said, he and his brother arriving with two different kinds of saddles in tow.

"But we couldn't get the bin full of other stuff," Brian said, adjusting his hold on his saddle.

"I can get it," Noel found himself saying.

"Oh, thank you," Monty said. "Could you close up the trailer too?"

"Sure thing," he said and was rewarded with a smile.

He jogged over to the truck and hefted out the large black bin from the back. *Dang. What did she have in here? Bricks?* He opened it and found leather straps and blankets on top. Curious, he moved the corner of one blanket and peeked beneath. Books on horses. Pamphlets about equestrian horse therapy. Peeking around and seeing no one watching, he folded one pamphlet and slipped it into his pocket.

After shoving the ramp back up into the horse trailer, he closed the door and carried the heavy crate across the parking lot and out onto the football practice field shared by both the high school and middle school.

Autumn this year was still ongoing and Northeast Ohio's weather was unseasonably warm for the first week of December, although snow was predicted over the weekend. Because of this, the career fair was being held outside, with various booths set up, including one for both the new electronics and microchip companies that had recently set up business in the area. Joe Hillis from the Knobs & Knockers had his on one side of the field, complete with different kinds of tools for kids to try under his supervision. Nick nodded his direction as he walked past with the crate.

A booth was set up that had two men and two women in various military uniforms seated at a table, sharing coffee. The new hospital booth held several people in scrubs. On their table was blood pressure cuffs, as well as stethoscopes and large posters with different kinds of hospital jobs hanging on the lattice walls of their booth. Even Mayor Maggie Lawson stood talking with the county's social worker in a booth with posters about the county's government programs.

As he passed those, he saw a large area that had been roped off. Sugarplum was grazing on the field, while Monty stood talking to Holly. He walked over and set the bin on the ground next to the foldup table each booth had for pamphlets and paraphernalia.

"Looks like it's going to be a very busy day out here," he said.

Holly grinned. "I'm glad the weather held long enough for us to have it outside. The basketball coaches and the principal nixed the idea of us having a horse on the newly refinished gymnasium floor. It being basketball season and all."

"Yeah, Nick said he'd been working overtime last month to get it fixed for the first tip-off. How are you all handling the kids? Aren't you worried someone might get hurt out here," he asked, nodding towards the mare, who was placidly nibbling on the field.

"Sugarplum is used to lots of kids," Monty said, opening the bin and removing the leather straps. Noel wondered what they were used for.

"Besides, they'll be coming out in small groups during their social study class," Holly said, shifting her weight and pressing her hand to the small of her back. "Cleetus is here for crowd control today, so my worst worry is how long I will be on my feet." She paused and fixed him with narrowed eyes. "Do not tell your brother that, or he'll be down here demanding I go lay down somewhere. He's gotten very overprotective with this baby, even more than last time."

"Mums the word, as long as you're okay. If not, I can't promise anything."

"I'm fine."

He glanced at his watch. "Speaking of my brother, I'd best get over to the job site or he's going to dock my pay."

Holly laughed. "He is a stickler for punctuality, although Gabriel is convincing him to be a little more lax about that, especially when it's Nick's turn to get him off to pre-school. Like this morning."

"Great! If I hurry, maybe I can beat him there. Have a good day," he said, giving her a kiss on the cheek. He turned to the redhead, "Nice to meet you, Monty."

"It was my pleasure, Noel," she said with a smile, then went back to unloading her supplies.

Dismissed.

And didn't that bruise his male ego just slightly? He sauntered back to the front parking lot musing on just how he should be thankful she wasn't interested in him with all the complications he had in his life. Between work with his brother in his new construction firm, trips out of the state or country when the Army or State Department needed him, and having a burgeoning teen daughter at home, the last thing he needed was a woman in his life. Albeit a very pretty woman. Trouble was, her disinterest had the opposite effect. He loved a challenge.

Chapter Two

"How's it going?" Holly asked Monty later that day, carrying out a tray with two sandwich boxes and fresh bottles of water from the cafeteria.

"Great," she answered as she finished giving Sugarplum some water in the portable thirteen gallon water trough. "You didn't have to bring me lunch."

Holly waved her off. "Part of the career day is lunch provided by the Peaches 'N Cream Café for all the people volunteering their time, as well as the teachers. Just because you have to stay outside with Sugarplum while everyone else gets a break, doesn't mean you shouldn't get a free lunch." She set the tray on the table next to the books and pamphlets, then pulled up one of the two chairs provided for each booth. "Besides, I was under strict orders from Lorna to *get off your feet for a while girl.*"

"Well, in that case, who am I to get you in trouble with Lorna? She might ban both of us from ever eating in the café again. And I do adore her pies."

They both laughed.

Monty took one of the to-go boxes and opened it to find a

chicken salad on croissant sandwich, along with a bag of chips and two big slices of blondie brownies. She took a healthy bite of the sandwich and moaned slightly at the flavor of chicken, celery, onions, pecan chips and dried cranberries in the mayonnaise-based dressing on the buttery homemade croissants everyone knew came from the Yeast & West Bakery in town.

After swallowing her mouthful and taking a long drink of water, she smiled at her friend. "Okay, I think I love this chicken salad as much as the pies. I've had it a few times for lunch when I've stopped in at the Peaches 'N Cream. But I've always been curious about the name of it. *Emma's chicken salad.* Why not Lorna's?"

A little less than a year ago, she'd moved to the area and was still getting used to not only a new home and job, but the quaintness of living in a smalltown community again. Growing up as the daughter of a teacher and steel production foreman on a family farm outside a small mill town in western Pennsylvania, she'd had two horses and ridden them in competitions. On her graduation, she headed out to the University of Pittsburgh to stretch her legs in a crowded city. It wasn't too far from her hometown, and yet gave her a chance to experience things she wouldn't have gotten living at home.

After receiving her Master's degree in therapeutic counseling, she'd taken a special training course in using horses to enhance that therapy. She believed horses could make a difference in people's lives. She'd experienced it herself. The horses she'd cared for, rode, and competed with had taken a shy girl who stuttered when speaking in public or in large groups and given her self-confidence, helping her to overcome that terribly embarrassing speech disorder.

For a while she worked on a ranch in Texas that specialized in using adaptive riding to aid individuals with disabilities to improve their life skills and independence. But she hated the heat of west Texas, missed the changing seasons she'd grown up with in the northeast. She'd wanted to move back home, but the farm was a family owned business she and her brothers inherited when their parents passed away. There wasn't enough space to add on an equine therapy facility.

So, she'd waited and saved her money until the news of a farm in the central northeast area of Ohio was for sale. The owners had passed away and their daughters lived on opposite coasts with their families. When she'd come to tour the farm in person, she'd loved the two-story farmhouse with the big front porch. But what really sold her was the large red barn and paddock area for horses, along with the tack—stirrups, saddles, reins, bridles, harnesses, bit and halters. Unfortunately, the horses themselves had been sold off separately, so her business plan had to include the purchase of horses. Sugarplum was the first she'd purchased, and that was from a ranch owner in Texas. Already trained, the mare gave her the ability to offer her services quickly the day she arrived in Westen.

"The reason it's called *Emma's Chicken Salad* and not Lorna's," Holly said, answering Monty's question, "is Emma Preston used to work at the café and she's the one who made the original recipe. It was such a hit, Lorna decided to give Emma credit for it when she added it permanently to the menu."

"Emma Preston? The twins mother?" she asked then took another bite.

Holly swallowed her mouthful and nodded. "Yes. She married Doc Clint when the twins were about six years old, then had two more children. She finished nursing school and now works with him at the clinic."

"I know Emma. She's come out with their church youth group to help work on the ranch." She chuckled. "She was surprised at how the idea of earning time riding the horses could motivate the kids—especially her sons—to muck out stalls with little complaint."

"I bet. Believe it or not, when they were younger, they were a bit of a terror. My niece even got into a fist fight with one of them."

"Sweet Callie?"

Holly nodded. "It was the Christmas I met Nick, the same year her mother died. She was new in town, and you know how eight-year old boys try to get a girl's attention."

"They tease them."

"Yes, and she didn't think their teasing was funny. I believe all three ended up with black eyes. Callie did swing first though." Holly chuckled. "Poor Nick. It was the first time he stood in for Noel, who'd been called into active duty and was out of the country at the time. He's a great uncle but was at his wits end on how to deal with his young niece. But he handled it well and they both survived. Now, it's like having a part-time daughter when she comes to stay with us."

"Does she do that often?"

"Stay with us? Only when Noel gets called up. He's a reservist with the Army and a linguist. Nick told me he speaks numerous languages, especially several dialects of Arabic. When his team is headed into a situation, they not only get a trained soldier, but an interpreter in the mix. In the five years since I married Nick, Callie's been with us seven times. Mostly short stints of a week or two."

"And when he's home, he works with Nick in the construction business?"

"Their father was a contractor when they were growing up and instead of doing nothing on school breaks, they worked with him on houses. Nick loved the carpentry parts and Noel gravitated to the electrical." She paused to drink half the bottle of water in front of her before continuing. "But their parents wanted them to serve in the military because they believed it taught them discipline and loyalty. Both of them joined the Army, but in different ways. Nick went right in after high school. Noel went to college as part of the ROTC."

"Was that when he learned the languages?" Monty asked, curious about the tall handsome man.

Holly nodded again. "According to Nick his brother just sort of stumbled into it. He hadn't graduated from college yet when he was approached to go to Iraq as an interpreter. After six months, he came back, finished his schooling and joined the Army, then went to Ranger school."

"Whoa."

Holly gave her the I-know-what-you-mean look.

Monty was truly impressed. What little she knew about the Rangers was they were the elite soldiers in the Army. Highly trained, both physically and mentally, they were sent on high-risk missions that others couldn't handle.

"Are they originally from Westen?" she couldn't help her curiosity about Holly's husband's family, especially his brother.

"No. Callie's mother was. They met at college and she lived in Columbus for the first few years of their marriage, even though he was overseas most of it."

"So how did they end up back here?"

"When Rebecca became pregnant, she wanted to be closer to her family. Both of her parents were still living then and could help her when Noel was deployed. They bought a house here and she started teaching in the local high school."

"Is that when Noel left the permanent military?" It wasn't really any of her business, but this man's story just drew her in.

Holly munched on one of the blondies from her lunch box. "No. He stayed in for the first six years of Callie's life. It was Rebecca's cancer diagnosis that brought him home."

Monty didn't ask any more questions about Noel as they

finished their lunches, the conversation turned to Holly's pregnancy and plans for the new baby's arrival.

"One of the kids today asked me if I was going to be part of the Yuletide Jubilee," Monty said as they were cleaning up their meal. "What exactly is that?"

"It's a weekend-long festival that Westen has been putting on since before World War Two. It started during the Depression. There's a holiday craft fair and all the downtown businesses have specials for the out-of-towners who come just for the quaintness of a small town during the holidays. And the pageant play will happen on Friday evening and Saturday and Sunday afternoons, with the tree lighting Friday night and a dinner-dance Saturday night. I've been working with the kids all of November to learn the music and the play."

"What play is it?"

Holly giggled. "The play itself is always a retelling of Dickens' *The Christmas Carol*. Except we use more modern day characters to tell it. We've used *The Wizard of Oz*, *Star Wars* and even *Sponge Bob* one year."

"And this year?"

"Superheroes."

"Who will be Scrooge?"

Holly shrugged with a bit of a mischievous grin. "It's a secret, that is if I can keep the kids from telling their parents." She stretched, pressing her fist to the small of her back as the end of lunch bell rang, signaling another group of kids would be heading out to the career fair. "The town council is having a planning meeting tonight. All the business owners, as well as the sheriff and fire chief will be there. You should come."

"Me? I don't think so."

"Sure you should. You have a new business in town."

"Technically, it's out of town."

"So is Mayor Maggie's tree farm and Christmas shop. She

always has a booth at the fair and advertises her business in the free town magazine given to all the visitors." Holly gathered up their trash and started to head back inside, then stopped to grin at her. "And one handsome electrician will be there to discuss all the lighting they'll string up over Main Street."

Chapter Three

"Wow, this place is packed," Nick said as he, Holly and Noel stepped inside the Westen Civic Center.

Noel was as surprised as his brother. In all the years since his family had moved to Westen, this was the first Yuletide Jubilee planning meeting he'd ever attended. Holly warned him when he dropped off Callie to babysit her cousin Gabe that the meeting would be well attended, but boy he hadn't expected standing room only.

At the table on the stage sat Mayor Maggie Landon, as well as Lorna Doone, the head of the town's chamber of commerce, Sheriff Gage Justice, Fire Chief Deke Reynolds and Colm Riley the county treasurer. There was one empty seat.

Noel moved to the side as Nick walked his very pregnant wife to the stage and offered her a hand up the stairs. Gage grabbed a second chair so Nick could sit near his wife on stage, which left Noel on his own. He leaned against the wall a moment and scanned the audience, looking for an empty chair. The town council and all the people on the stage had already had a preliminary meeting. Tonight was an open session for any citizen to attend and hear the plans for the town's biggest event of every year. From what Noel could see every business in the downtown area was represented, along with the local farmers. Even the new hospital and school administrators were in the audience.

The history of the jubilee went all the way back to the Depression. The story was told to every new resident about how during the hardest times, the town came together to support the farmers who were having trouble selling their crops and home-made goods because customers couldn't afford to buy them. The mayor at the time came up with the idea to hold a country fair where town folks and other people could come and exchange homemade crafts and canned goods. Everyone who attended was asked to pay a minimum of a quarter per person. The local restaurants and churches made dinner for anyone who attended. The school children put on a pageant play all three nights of the jubilee. On the last night of the event, the mayor and town council counted up all the proceeds and discovered they'd made over ten thousand dollars.

Noel had asked Holly what they'd done with the money.

"*They opened a community soup kitchen. It served hot meals twice a day throughout that winter,*" *Holly said. "The story is that had they not provided families with food that winter, many would've starved to death. The next year, the same thing happened, but that time it was enough money to help some of the families keep their homes. In fact, since then, every year, the jubilee brings in more money and the town divides the proceeds up between the civic functions. After-school care for kids and athletic equipment for the high school, meals for shut-ins and the elderly. Even free healthcare once a week over at the clinic.*"

The door beside Noel opened and the red-headed horse owner, Monty, stepped inside. She glanced his way with a little smile, then scanned the room the same way he'd just done.

"It's standing room only," he said and scooted away from the door to make room for her to lean against the wall beside him. For a moment, he thought she'd go the opposite direction, but relaxed when she moved in beside him.

"Did I miss anything?" she asked in a whisper.

He shook his head. "No, we just got here and apparently they were waiting for Holly to arrive."

As if on cue, Mayor Maggie stood at the podium. "I want to welcome everyone to this year's Yuletide Jubilee planning meeting. For those of you who are new, I hope you've read the article in the newspaper or on the town's website about the history of the Yuletide Jubilee and what its tradition means to Westen. We're very glad you're here and hope you'll enthusiastically participate in many or all of the events."

The meeting progressed as each person on the stage gave a report regarding their responsibilities for the weekend's plans. When Holly rose to talk about the children's play and announced this year would be superheroes, laughter and applause rippled through the audience.

"She's very good at that," Monty said.

Noel leaned a little closer, as much to sample the scent of her as much as to hear her over the applause. "What do you mean?"

"Inspiring people, making them laugh and relax. Making her ideas for the play sound like something they'll all want to get behind."

He smiled as he watched his little sister-in-law waddle back to her seat. "Yeah. I think she's been great for my brother. She really helped Callie deal with the grief after her mother died and I was out of the country."

"I tried to get Holly to tell me which character was going to be Scrooge, but she wouldn't."

"Me either."

Her blue eyes widened in surprise. "You don't even know?"

"Nope and she's sworn all the kids to secrecy. Trust me, I tried to get it out of Callie, but no luck."

"She wants to surprise the audience. I'm thinking we'll figure it out if suddenly there's a run on green material over at the quilt store."

"You might be right. That would be a hulking big scrooge." He laughed, then realized his brother had just called his name. "Looks like I'm up."

He pushed away from the wall and headed to the stage to discuss the plans for lighting the Christmas tree in the town square, as well as along the main streets of town, and the number of volunteers he'd need this weekend to get them up for the holiday season. But he'd much rather continue the whispered conversation with Monty.

*
* *

"Trying to decide where to volunteer?" the deep voice said from behind her.

Monty swallowed her smile, turned, and shook her head. "I'm not sure I'm a fit for any of them."

Noel blinked. "None? There are dozens of opportunities." He leaned past her, to pick up a clipboard. "How about helping decorate gingerbread houses at the craft fair?"

She laughed. "I haven't an artistic bone in my body."

"That can't be true. Everyone has some sort of creative talent."

"No. Honestly. My stick figures don't even look like stick figures."

He laughed and the deep sound sent waves of pleasure over her. She'd made him do that.

"Okay," he said, moving down to the next clipboard. "How about baking cookies for the school play's bake sale?"

"I don't bake."

He looked at her incredulously. "Not even Christmas cookies?"

She shook her head. "Nope. I spent so little time in the kitchen growing up that my mother just focused on teaching me the basics so I wouldn't starve to death as an adult. I can grill a steak or burger, make a salad, mac and cheese from a box, and oatmeal for breakfast. Otherwise, my kitchen is rarely used. And never for baking."

"So you don't eat Christmas cookies?" he asked setting the clipboard back on the table and moved to the next one.

"Oh, I eat them. I just don't bake them. They'd probably end up burnt to a crisp or taste like wallpaper."

He laughed again and picked up the next list. "Okay, how about this one: strolling Christmas caroling. It's fun. You get to dress up in an old fashioned costume and wander around singing Christmas carols for the tourists."

"Tone deaf."

"Now you're just making up excuses," he said, setting the list down and lifting one eyebrow in skepticism at her.

She shook her head. "Nope. Can't carry a tune in a bucket."

"That's sad."

"It is. I love listening to them, but only sing them around the horses. They don't seem to mind how off tune I am, or at least they don't complain."

"Okay, let's try one more," he said, reaching for the final sign-up sheet at the end of the table. "Manning the ice-skating rink."

She shook her head. "Weak ankles."

"Guess you wouldn't be able to rescue anyone who falls on the ice then," he said as they headed for the exit.

21

"I'd probably land on top of them."

Once more he laughed and this time she smiled. She liked the jovial conversation and his teasing her. Unlike her brothers and some other men she'd known in her life, he didn't do it to embarrass her or hurt her feelings.

"You could always come help string lights tomorrow. I assume you can climb a ladder, or are you afraid of heights?"

"No, but I have several clients with disabilities coming for riding sessions tomorrow and Saturday. If the weather turns like the weathermen are suggesting, it may be their last chance to get on a horse outside for a while."

They stepped out into the dark night and were hit with colder air than when they'd arrived earlier. "Dang that cold front is moving in a little faster than anticipated. I guess Ohio has decided to get ready for winter."

She shivered and zipped her jacket up to her neck. "I hope the snow holds off until Sunday."

He shoved his hands into his coat pocket as they headed for the parking lot. "Callie was telling me about how you have two kinds of horse therapy. One for troubled teens or adults and another for kids with disabilities. How does that work?"

"It depends on what disabilities the client has. By the way, it's not just kids with disabilities, but teens and adults can benefit from it too."

"What benefits do they get?"

"One way is physically the rhythm of the horse's gait moves the client's body in a way that's similar to a human gait. It can improve their posture, flexibility, balance and strengthen their muscles."

"Wow. Do you see results immediately?"

"No, it comes with time and repetitive riding sessions. We've been lucky with the weather so far this year that we haven't had to postpone any lessons. After this weekend, we'll have no outdoor riding sessions until March and then only if the weather holds."

"Isn't that going to stress your income?" he asked as they neared her pickup truck.

She clicked the button to unlock it and opened the door. He held it open as she climbed in, almost as if he didn't want their conversation to end. It had been a long time since a man seemed to actually be interested in what she had to say, not just give her a patronizing explanation of why she didn't know anything. But Noel listened.

"I've been saving for years to have my own horse farm and therapy practice. Along with what my parents left me in their wills, I've been able to plan for the winter break. But it's only the outdoor riding sessions that will be on hold. We have an indoor riding arena, so lessons will move inside for the winter. We also provide lodging and care for other horse owners who don't have the space to do it themselves. Then we have clients who come to help care for the animals as part of their therapy for things like anxiety, trauma, depression, even PTSD."

"I'd love to learn more about that."

"You should bring Callie out to the farm, and I can show you what we do."

"She'd love that. I've heard nothing but horses since she turned thirteen."

Monty laughed. "That's the age that I fell in love with them too. If you want to bring her by after school tomorrow, she can watch one of our sessions."

"If we get enough done on the town lighting tomorrow, I just might."

She started the engine, then pulled one of her business cards from the storage compartment between the seats. "Give me a call if you're coming and I'll be sure she gets a chance to get involved. Maybe even get on a horse."

"I'll do that," he said, taking the card and stepping back so she could close the door.

She waved and put the truck in reverse. From her rearview mirror she saw him watch her leave, still holding the card in his hands. For some reason that made her feel special, like he was responsible for her getting safely on the road. Which was ridiculous. From the day she'd left home, she'd been the only one responsible for her welfare.

Shaking off the odd sensation, she turned onto the road that led out of town toward her farm. She hoped he'd take advantage of that card and call her. It would be good for his daughter to not only fulfill her dream of working with horses, but to see how it helps others. If she was honest with herself though, she'd have to admit she wouldn't mind seeing the handsome man once more and hearing his laugh.

Chapter Four

"Sorry I'm a little late," Noel said as he pulled into the student pickup spot the next afternoon and Callie climbed into the passenger seat, her cheeks flushed pink from the wintery wind blowing through the town.

"That's okay," she said as she fastened her seatbelt. "Mrs. Tacket let me sit in the office and do my homework, which wasn't much. Then I helped her print up the fliers for the play all the students are going to hand out starting Monday. They're really cool."

"Glad you got to help do something for the Jubilee. That's why I was late," he said pulling out onto the main road, but not heading towards their home. "I wanted to get as much work done early on the street lighting, so we could do something special this evening."

That got her attention.

"What?" she asked, sitting a little straighter and curiosity filling her face.

He chuckled. "You'll see."

Keeping his eyes on the GPS on the dashboard, he maneuvered through the side streets to the main highway that led east of town then turned right heading south into the older farm country that the new development of Westen hadn't encroached on yet. The slate grey skies signaled the snow expected for the weekend might be coming early.

At a farm road, the GPS said to turn right again, and he hid his smile as they drove past the white fences and through the gate that said, Gentle Creek Ranch over the entrance.

"Oh my gosh! Oh my gosh, Daddy!" Callie bounced in her seat and squealed beside him, sounding more like his little girl than a sullen teenager.

He chuckled as he drove past the barn and corral area. Horses wandered about freely in the pasture beyond them. Finally, he stopped in front of the charming, two-story, red-roofed, white farmhouse where Monty, with a black and white Border Collie by her side, stood on the large porch that extended across the entire front. For someone who confessed she didn't do many Christmas things, she'd decorated each column of the porch with greenery wreaths bearing large red bows. If he was a painter or a photographer, he'd use this image to make Christmas cards, especially if the snow they were promised arrived.

Callie had her seatbelt unsnapped before he put the SUV in park.

"Slow down, sweetheart," he said, climbing out of the vehicle. "I know you're excited..." his words trailing off as she'd already bounded up the steps to the porch talking to Monty.

He shook his head, shoved his hands in the pockets of his coat and joined them.

"I just can't believe Dad is letting me come and help with the horses," Callie was saying.

Whoa. He hadn't made any such promise. He'd better set the record straight.

"What I think your father has agreed to, is for you to see

how we use the horses in a therapy session and then how we care for the horses afterwards," Monty said before he could, giving him a knowing look.

"Yes, but I really want to train horses," Callie said, her voice including a little bit of whine but still enthusiastic.

"Why don't we let Miss Taylor show us around," he said, watching his daughter's posture slump slightly in disappointment, "and we'll see how you do or don't like working on the ranch. Okay?"

"Okay," his daughter said, but didn't accompany it with an eye-roll. *Progress.*

"Let's start at the barn where Beth is having a therapy session." Monty motioned for them to head back down the porch steps, the dog bounding along beside them.

"What's his name?" Callie asked, matching Monty stride for stride.

"Rufus. He's a guard dog to keep predators from hurting the horses." Monty said.

Noel walked slightly behind the pair, scanning the area on their trek. "Your barn is larger than I thought most are."

"It's because this isn't just a barn for the horses," Monty said with a laugh. "The previous owner had show horses. Apparently, their daughters were into dressage."

"What's dressage?" Callie asked.

"It's a competition type of horse riding where the horse and rider have to learn and execute specific kinds of maneuvers to exact specifications. It's an Olympic sport."

"Is it like barrel racing?"

Monty laughed. "No, it's more like horse dancing. But it does take a lot of training, so the previous owners built a training arena and barn system which benefits my therapy business. It allows me to offer indoor sessions when the weather gets bad or too cold for the riders to be outside."

"And too cold for the horses too?" Callie asked.

"Actually, horses do well in cold, even snowy weather, as long as it isn't too wet, too windy or below about twenty degrees." Monty opened the door and they stepped into what looked like a big open arena.

The scent of horses, hay and a faint hint of manure hit Noel immediately. Callie didn't seem to mind. Her eyes lit up at the site of the horse on the far side of the arena where a young man, a woman, and a girl with what looked like a bicycle helmet stood talking. "Oh, there's Sugarplum!"

"Yes. She's the horse Beth has been riding in her sessions. That's her and her mother," Monty said as they walked that way on the outside of the fenced in area. "Camden is one of my horse trainers and is studying equestrian therapy at Kent State."

Monty stopped them a few feet from the trio and the horse. Noel realized that Beth had Down's Syndrome. She held onto Sugarplum's lead and stroked her muzzle, staring into the horse's eyes as if the two of them were having their own private conversation.

"One of the first things we encourage our clients to do is touch the horses so they won't be afraid of something twice their height," Monty said, her voice lowered. "Often some of them have trust issues with people but build a bond with the horse much easier." She leaned closer to Callie. "Sugarplum is one of the best for bonding with scared or shy people like Beth."

An older man walked into the arena from a side door carrying what looked like a set of three steps and set in next to Sugarplum. Then he said something to Beth, who grinned up at him and nodded. She released the horse's reins to him. He steadied the horse while Camden helped her mount and settle comfortably in the saddle before handing the reins back to her.

"What's Camden holding?" Callie asked, pointing to the rope attached to the horse's halter.

The stable hand held it loosely as he led Sugarplum and Beth around the arena. Her mother and the older man slowly walked towards Monty, Callie and Noel.

"It's a lead rope or guide rope," Monty explained. "Beth is learning to use the reins to control Sugarplum, but for safety's sake Camden will walk along with her using the guide rope to be sure Sugarplum knows where to go. Inside like this, there isn't a lot to distract her, but outside we don't want her taking off with Beth on her back until she's confident of controlling the horse."

"When will that be?"

Monty considered her words. "For some of our clients it takes a few months or even years. Unfortunately, sometimes they can never accomplish that skill. But being in complete control of the horse isn't necessarily the only goal."

"It's not?"

"No," Beth's mother said, coming to stand beside them and lean on the railing to watch her daughter. "Beth was so shy when we started her therapy four months ago, she couldn't talk to anyone but me and her father. Sugarplum broke through that barrier. For her, the ability to speak to others is a very big achievement."

"Besides communication there are all kinds of other benefits from workin' with and ridin' horses," the older man sporting a thick salt and pepper mustache said with a decided western accent. Noel was reminded of a famous western actor. "Self-confidence, trust in others, leadership. Gives them strength, balance, and develops core muscles in the body. I once saw a young man who couldn't sit straight in his wheelchair eventually be able to sit in a regular saddle after months of ridin' sessions."

"This is Mrs. Watters, Beth's mom, and my foreman, Bruce Hill," Monty introduced the pair. "This is Noel Fisher and his daughter Callie. They're here for a tour of the facilities and what we do here."

"Glad to meet you," Noel said, shaking hands with Mrs. Watters and Bruce.

"Bruce and I worked on a therapy ranch in west Texas," Monty said. "When I bought this farm, he agreed to come help me get it going."

"Someone had to be sure you weren't buying a pig in a poke," the foreman said with a wink.

Monty gave him a sardonic look. "I asked you to come because I didn't think you could stay out of trouble if I left you down there alone."

Callie laughed with Beth's mother.

"Is riding the only part of the therapy sessions?" Noel asked, attempting to rescue his fellow male from being picked on by the women. That it drew Monty's attention to him was just a bonus.

"Once the client gets comfortable with their mount, we encourage them to participate in their care," Monty said.

"Like what?" Callie asked.

"Grooming. And feeding them in winter. In the spring, summer and fall we turn out the horses for the day so they can graze as much as they want."

"What's turn out?"

"That's letting the horses roam freely to graze in the pastures. Horses like to move about and need lots of room for that. It keeps their muscles and joints working properly. We only bring them inside for sessions and at night to their stalls for protection. And of course, in the winter when it is too cold, wet or windy."

"Wow, there's a lot to know about horses," Callie said, sounding both impressed and surprised.

"How does grooming add to your clients' therapies?" Noel

30

asked, leaning on the rail like Bruce to watch Beth and her therapist put the horse through what looked like a special routine, a slow walk around the entire oval arena area and then a little faster half-way around and repeat. The joy on the young girl's face was infectious.

"It gives Beth a chance to care for Sugarplum," her mother replied, her gaze fixed on her daughter. "It also teaches her responsibility, let's her show compassion for another creature, helps her have less fear in the horse. They've bonded well, not just because of the riding, but the hands-on care Beth gives her horse."

Suddenly the lights in the paddock flickered, then went out.

"Dagnabit," Bruce muttered. "The circuit done blew a fuse again."

"Beth, don't be frightened," Monty called out, pulling out her phone and turning on the flashlight app and held it out to shine light on her client. "Camden is going to walk you and Sugarplum over here, okay?"

"Okay, Ms. Monty. Sugarplum wasn't scared, so I wasn't either."

"That's the third time this month, Bruce," Monty said.

"I know, Boss. Gonna go through all those new fuses we bought at this rate," the foreman replied, flicking on his own phone's flashlight and walked away.

"Mind if I go with you?" Noel asked, striding to catch up with him.

"Know anything about fuses?" Bruce asked.

"Kind of. I'm an electrician."

Bruce stopped and grinned at him. "Well, now. Ain't that fortuitous. I've been fightin' this old barn's electrical ever since the day Monty bought the place."

"When was that?" Noel asked as they continued to the back of the building.

"She purchased it back in June, but we didn't get out here until the end of July. Took a while to get the horses ready for travel."

"Do you have any idea when this place was built?"

Bruce opened a door and they stepped into a storeroom of sorts. He picked a vintage glass fuse out of the open box on what looked like a work bench. "I believe it was in the nineteen-fifties. You'd have to check with the boss to get the exact year."

Noel held the light for the other man as he replaced the fuse, then flipped the lever to turn the power back on.

The room flooded with light.

"That do it, Boss?" the foreman yelled out the door.

"Everything's on again," she called back.

Noel stepped closer to the fuse box. He took his flashlight and looked closely at the wiring going from the box. "This looks like it's never been updated to meet current code."

"I was afraid of that," Monty's voice said from the doorway.

He looked over his shoulder at her watching him worriedly.

"I left Callie with Beth's mom while Beth finishes her therapy session," she said stepping into the small room.

"You've got some old wiring back here." Noel shined his light on the problem spot, hidden behind the box. "Do you have a rodent problem?"

"We did have rats when we first moved into the place," Monty said. "I bought several cats from one of the Amish farmers. They're good mousers and seemed to have curtailed the problem to a manageable state. Why?"

He pointed to the where the cloth rapping on the wire looked like something had been nibbling on it. "Cloth wiring is good insulation as long as it isn't damaged. Seems like something was snacking on this. If that's causing you to blow the fuses, it should be fixed immediately, or you run the risk of a barn fire."

"How much is that going to cost?" she asked as she leaned in to view the wiring, concern in her voice.

"You should probably replace the entire fuse box too. So, I'd say whatever the cost of the wires and box. I'll have to check with Joe over at the Knobs & Knockers."

Monty chuckled, stepping back.

"What?" he asked with a bit of a grin, glad to see the worry gone from her beautiful face.

"The name of the hardware store makes me laugh."

"I laughed the first time Nick sent me there for supplies."

They stood staring at each other for a moment, then her cheeks filled with color and she broke the contact. "So, if we change out the box, the fire risk will be gone?"

"The immediate threat, yes."

"What does that mean?"

He turned off his flashlight and pocketed his phone, hesitating before giving her the bad news. "If the previous owners ignored updating the fuse box and wiring in here, it's safe to say they made no updates to any of the wiring throughout the entire facility, and there might be frayed wires anywhere along them from the rats."

"Which means there could be old, frayed wiring hidden anywhere," she heaved a sigh, "or everywhere."

"Afraid so."

She shook her head and exited back into the training area, Noel and Bruce following her. "Well, isn't that a great Christmas gift? I'm pretty sure it's going to cost more than what I have in savings."

"You could always get a personal loan, or maybe sell your portion of the family farm to your brothers?" Bruce suggested.

Shaking her head, she stopped to watch Beth making another trip around the arena. "No, the farm is just above water again for them right now, so I can't ask either of them to go in the red to pay me."

"Well, this place burns to the ground, Boss and you'll be out more money than it's worth."

"I get that, Bruce."

"I was just sayin'," her foreman said, sounding a little hurt.

Monty reached out and squeezed his shoulder. "You aren't saying anything that isn't true, old friend. As they say down in Texas, you shoot straight from the hip. It's what I like about you and why I asked you to come work for me."

Noel liked how the older man deferred to her and how she respected his opinion. He also saw how his news weighed on them both. "Before you go off to the bank or approach your family, why don't you let me get you an estimate of the cost of the material needed to do the job? First things first, I'll fix the fuse box, since we know it needs to be dealt with immediately. That won't be too costly. Then we'll look at what it would take to bring the whole place up to code."

"You'll need to add the estimate for labor too," Monty said, slipping her hands into the back pockets of her jeans as they walked back to where Callie and Beth's mother stood.

With great determination, Noel focused on her face and not how her actions arched her back and thrust her breasts slightly forward against the plaid shirt and insulated vest. Lusting over a potential client wasn't a very good idea. Especially one who offered to let his daughter indulge in her newfound love of horses.

"I'll fix the fuse box for just the cost of materials, since that's the immediate problem."

"I can't let you do that," she said, stopping and fixing him with a look that suggested he'd somehow wounded her pride.

"How about you give Callie a few riding lessons for free and we'll call the labor cost for the repair even."

"I don't think—"

"What's to think about?" Bruce interrupted her. "The man's daughter wants to learn to ride. You have horses. You need someone to repair the fuse box. The man's an electrician. It needs to be fixed before a fire breaks out or the fire chief comes to do the annual inspection and closes the whole place down."

Monty stopped and shot him a slant-eyed look that her foreman just shrugged off.

"I'm just sayin'," he muttered and walked ahead of them.

Noel had no idea if annual inspections were done on private farms or not but had the good sense to keep his mouth shut.

"How long will it take you to do the fuse box repair?" she asked.

"Shouldn't take me more than an hour or so."

"Aren't you supposed to be doing the lighting on main street this weekend?"

She'd remembered what he was doing for the Jubilee. She'd been paying attention. That felt nice. Not since his wife could he remember a woman noticing his movements. At least not one whose movements he also noticed.

"Noel?" she asked, and he realized he'd never answered.

"I am. We got a lot done today and tomorrow's work is already laid out so it should be done before evening. I could pick up the new box and wiring while I'm in town, then come out after we finish up, if that would work for you?"

"Sure."

They stood watching Beth ride around the training arena. Noel's gaze automatically went to his daughter, her face filled with joy at watching the horse. "Do you have clients scheduled for therapy sessions tomorrow?"

"I did. But given the state of the fuse box, I think I'll spend my evening rescheduling them. After Beth finishes, we'll turn off all the power out here. Bruce might think I don't understand the severity of the situation, but I would hate for anyone, human or animal, to be hurt in a fire." She paused and glanced around the facility. "Do I need to wait until all the re-wiring is completed before I have clients here?"

The heaviness of that question spoke volumes. This was her livelihood. He suspected she'd poured all she had into purchasing the place and getting her therapy program started. The unforeseen cost of the electrical repairs was problem enough. If she had to shut down her program for too long, would she ever recoup the lost income?

"I tell you what," he said wanting to ease some of her burden. "Reschedule your clients for the weekend only. Once the fuse box is repaired, I'll check out the rest of the system and we'll know exactly how to go from there."

Nodding, she stared off to one side, her lips pressed tight as she swallowed hard several times. She was fighting her emotions and he suspected tears. The urge to pull her into his arms and hold her close surprised him. Pretty sure she wouldn't appreciate a near stranger doing that, either.

"Will the horses be okay out here with the temperature falling tonight?" he asked to give her something else to focus on.

She laughed. "Horses are tougher than most people think. In the winter they put on a thick coat and do better outside where they can move around. We just need to be sure they have plenty of food and water. They'll be fine, even in the few inches of snow they're saying we'll get tonight, as long as it doesn't get below twenty degrees or it rains before it snows."

"What will you do if that happens?"

"Bring them inside here and blanket them."

Suddenly, Callie broke away from the fencing and ran their direction.

"Dad, can I help Beth groom Sugarplum? Mr. Bruce said I could," she said grinning hopefully at him.

"I don't see why not. But then we have to head home."

"Yes!" she said, pumping her fist down in victory and darted back to where Beth was dismounting her ride.

Monty laughed. "Oh, you're in trouble."

"Yeah, I know." He huffed out a sigh. "I guess I should be happy it's horses, not boys."

"Oh, that will come, but lucky for you not until she's older, and probably mature enough to handle it."

"Oh great."

Chapter Five

The bell above the door jangled and the dark-haired man seated at the counter looked over his shoulder to see who entered the café, something he'd been doing since the moment he sat down.

"Is there anything else I can get you?" Lorna Doone, owner of the Peaches 'N Cream Café asked as she filled his coffee mug, then flipped a mug over and filled it in front of Deputy Sheriff Jason Clarke as he took a seat two stools down from the stranger. "Maybe a slice of pie?"

The man shook his head and seemed to slump over his coffee. "No, thank you."

"Don't know what you're missing," Jason said. "Lorna's pies are legendary. Truckers have been known to make an extra stop in town just to get a slice. My favorite is cherry, but that's out of season. What's your favorite?"

The man glanced his way, straightened a little, then looked over at the glass-enclosed old-fashioned desert case. "Got any apple?"

"Sure do. You want it with or without cinnamon ice cream?" Lorna asked.

"Uhm, with, I guess."

"Make that two, Miss Lorna," Jason said with his usual good-natured grin. "Put them both on my ticket."

The man shook his head. "I got this."

"I'm sure you do." Jason took a long drink of his black coffee, then set the mug to the side. "But I pretty much talked you into it, so I might as well pay for them. Just small town friendliness. And we're pretty proud of the Peaches 'N Cream."

"It's a nice place," the stranger said.

"Best in the Midwest," Lorna said, setting two plates of apple pie alamode in front of them.

"I'm Jason," the youngest deputy in the sheriff's department said as he tucked into his food.

"Brody," the other man said, following suit on his desert.

Lorna moved down the counter, spraying down the nineteen-fifty's era Formica countertops she'd kept in excellent condition since the day she and her late husband had acquired the café, listening to the two men enjoy her pies. Sometimes she got more information on a person by just listening.

Brody seemed to be one of those lost souls that periodically wandered into Westen. Often, they weren't too friendly, but turned out to just need a helping hand. Sometimes though the strangers weren't friendly because they had nefarious plans. She'd learned over the years to welcome newcomers cautiously.

Jason had a way with people, which was one of the reasons he was such a good deputy. He might get more out of the man than she would.

"You new to Westen or just passing through?" Jason asked between bites.

"Just passing through, I guess." Brody stopped to take a drink of his coffee. "Looking for some work."

Jason, finished with his desert, turned on his stool to study the other man. "Westen's growing, that's for sure. Plenty of jobs. What experience do you have?"

"I was in the military for sixteen years." Brody finished his food and wiped his mouth. "Before that, high school. So, not much real world experience. I don't mind manual labor and I'm used to hard work."

"There's lots of construction going on if you've got any skills. Manual labor jobs are popping up on the local farms, as well as all the new businesses. Mayor Landon's office has a list of openings. Then there's always the sheriff's office. We could use more help that's for sure." Jason pulled out his wallet and handed Brody a card. "You can call and talk to Sheriff Justice if you're interested."

Brody's brows lifted and for the first time his lips quirked upwards slightly as if he wanted to smile but had forgotten how to. "Sheriff Justice."

Lorna relaxed. A man who could see the humor in their sheriff's last name certainly had potential. Picking up the tub of dirty dishes below the counter, she carried them past the pair. "You two finish up and I'll have your checks. Closing time is long past."

"Sorry, Ms. Lorna. Can I get a to-go cup on the coffee?" Jason asked, pulling out his wallet once more. "Don't forget, Brody's pie is on me."

Lorna set the tub of dishes down next to the sink where Danny, one of the local teens stood washing. "That's the last one," she said.

The lanky teen grinned at her. "That's good. I think my hands are gonna shrivel up from all this hot water."

"I told you to wear the rubber gloves," she said.

He held his hands up out of the soapy water to show her the yellow gloves. "I am. They're too big and keep slipping down and letting the water get in them."

"We'll get you some new ones tomorrow," Lorna said, shaking her head as she stepped back out to give the last two customers their checks.

Glenna, her long time waitress, had just flipped the closed sign and turned out the lights nearest the windows. Years ago, Lorna had learned that if she kept the lights on, locals and some travelers would assume she was open even if the sign was turned. Of course, she'd always let them in and served them, but she didn't like keeping her staff up late. They had families after all.

After the two men had paid and exited, she locked the front door and headed back to the kitchen. Danny walked out pushing the mop bucket, his head bouncing to the music playing through his earbuds.

"That boy's the cheeriest cleaner you've ever hired," Glenna said, closing out the register and bringing the cash drawer into the office.

Lorna nodded, taking the cash drawer from her. "The boy's motivated. His dad told him he couldn't get his driver's license until he had saved up the money to pay for half of a used car."

"Smart man," Pete said as he washed his hands.

For a man who looked like he'd climbed out of the Appalachian Mountains right after the Civil War—lean frame, long grey hair he kept pulled back in a ponytail and a grey beard —Pete was meticulous about his grill, prep knifes, kitchen and his hands. Many of the young kids that worked in the café over the years had learned from him the rules for running a kitchen to meet state inspection standards, and more importantly, his.

Pete was one of those lost souls who wandered into the Peaches 'N Cream that just needed a chance. She hadn't wanted to hire him, but her late husband recognized the army unit patch on his jacket and realized they might have served in Vietnam at the same time. From that moment on there hadn't been a question. Pete was coming to work at the café. Lorna learned something that day and took it to heart. You can't judge a book by its cover, and you have to give people a chance to show you who they are, good or bad.

"You think that new feller'll work out?" Pete asked, standing in the doorway to her office.

"Maybe. Depends on if he shows up tomorrow."

"Probably gonna sleep in his car tonight," he muttered as he walked away.

Lorna couldn't argue with him. Desperate people do desperate things. She should know.

Chapter Six

Around one the next afternoon, Noel stared down from the ladder where he'd just finished hanging the last Christmas lights on the south side of Main Street. Below, his team of workers milled about like worker ants. Despite the cold air that descended on the area last night and the two inches of snow they'd woken up to, his crew had worked steadily since eight in the morning.

It was his third time helping with the town's Yuletide Jubilee—his first as the lighting coordinator—yet he was still surprised at how many town folk showed up to help with the decorating. Everyone smiled, seemed genuinely happy to help and rarely did they give a grumpy word. Well, Harriett—he glanced her way to see the spry septuagenarian directing a group of teen boys in the process of cleaning up empty decoration boxes from the staging area with the countenance of a drill sergeant—always had a dry observation about something. But then, the woman always spoke like that so it couldn't be counted as a complaint.

During a break, he'd wandered over to the Knob & Knockers to purchase a new breaker box, one roll of the white PVC coated NM—nonmetallic wiring cable—and new junction boxes. He didn't know how many outlets were in Monty's barn facility, but he suspected he'd need at least a dozen to begin with.

He'd told her changing out the fuse box wouldn't be a big production. Even so, she'd struggled with the cost for just the small job. After he and Callie had eaten and she'd gone to bed, the problem of the barn's electrical issues nagged at him. This morning he'd made the decision. Whether or not she liked it, Monty was getting all the electrical in the place brought up to code, cost be damned.

Callie wanted to learn about horses and riding. She'd be spending a lot of time in that barn. It was his responsibility to see she was safe. The fact he'd also get to see more of the beautiful woman certainly hadn't played much in his decision making.

"You planning to stay up there all winter?" His brother Nick called from below.

He'd replaced the teenager who'd been steadying the ladder for him.

"Just checking how it looks from up here," he said, tightening the extra wire he'd used to secure the lights to the pole.

His six years of winter in the central northeastern Ohio town taught him you never counted on the weather to cooperate with the town's holiday plans. The sun could be shining and the temperatures mild to even warm one day, then a cold front could roll in from the west, the north or the east causing temps to plummet to below freezing the next. Even in early December it wasn't uncommon to end up with several inches of snow on the ground, like this morning.

The effect turned Westen and the surrounding area into one of those Currier & Ives Christmas card prints that drew even more tourists to the area. Bad weather was good for business in the small town. His job was to ensure all the decorations remained in place and no one was injured by a string of lights suddenly dropping from its mooring on the light poles.

So, he double checked the lights' security, then started back down the ladder. "When did you get here? Aren't you finishing that bathroom remodel up on Cherry Street today?" he asked when he stepped onto the sidewalk, where the snow had already evaporated except in the shadowed areas.

"Got finished early and the check is in my pocket," his brother said patting his coat. "Holly got a hankering for Pete's meatloaf and sent me to the Peaches 'N Cream for a to-go box."

"I thought she was busy making cookies with Callie and her friends today?" That's what his daughter said they were doing while he was supervising the street decorations.

Nick nodded. "That's what she said she was up to when I called home from the job site an hour ago. Apparently, the girls baked and decorated dozens of cookies for the school bake sale. My very pregnant wife is too dead on her feet to cook dinner."

Noel narrowed his eyes at his brother. "I thought meatloaf was on Tuesdays?"

"It is," Nick said with a grin. "I called to put in the order and was told it was unavailable. So, I asked to talk to Pete directly, explained that Holly was craving it."

"And Pete, the old softy is making her a meatloaf."

"Yep. Gonna buy the whole thing which means I get meatloaf sandwiches for lunch this week."

Noel slapped his arm around his brother and hugged him. "Something tells me, Holly wasn't the only one craving meatloaf."

"Don't tell my wife, but Pete's is the best I've ever eaten, including Holly's and Mom's."

Noel had to agree. Now he was wishing it was Tuesday so

he could have some. He picked up his toolbox and headed for his truck.

"You want to stay for dinner when you pick up Callie?" Nick asked, walking along beside him.

"Thanks for the offer, but she and I have an appointment later this afternoon." He set his toolbox inside the bed of his truck, strapping it in place and placing a lock on the strap. Westen might be a small town, but he wasn't leaving thousands of dollars of tools loose for anyone to just walk away with. Along with a strong work ethic, his father instilled the sense of responsibility for their equipment in both his sons.

"What project are you starting?" Nick asked, his brows lowered in confusion. "I don't recall us putting in any new bids or signing any new contracts. We have enough indoor work scheduled to keep the crews busy through the end of March."

"It's more of a favor than a job," he said opening his driver's side door. He took off his work gloves and set them in the box on the back seat, then reached for his driving gloves on the console between the front seats, not really wanting to have his brother quiz him over his plans.

"A favor?" Nick asked leaning up against the side of the truck, staring at him with that I'm-not-going-to-stop-asking-so-you-might-as-well-spill-it look.

"It's a simple job for Monty out at her place."

"Monty, huh?" Nick said with a grin in his voice.

Noel didn't give into the immature desire to slug his brother. Thankfully, they'd grown out of that stage two decades ago. "You know how horse-crazy Callie is. We went out to check out the lady's therapy business and the facilities. The lights went out while we were there. When I saw how old the fuse box was and how something, probably mice, had been chewing on the wiring, Monty told me she hadn't had the place checked out since she bought it. Looks to me like nothing was updated since it was built back in the fifties."

Nick let out a low whistle. "How big a favor is this going to be?"

"She agreed to let me fix the fuse box issue, in exchange for a riding lesson or two for Callie."

"I see. A swap then."

"Yes."

Nick glanced back into the truck bed. "Looks like you've got a lot of wire to do a simple job."

"If my daughter's going to be hanging out in that old barn, I'm going to be sure it isn't a fire hazard."

Nick started to say something more, but his phone suddenly buzzed in his coat pocket. He pulled it out and glanced at the message. "Love to stick around and hear more about your little project, but Pete's got my meatloaf ready."

They exchanged a brief hug and he jogged across the street.

"You'd better add some pie with that order," Noel called out after him. Nick grinned and waved.

Noel climbed into the truck and let the engine warm a few minutes, taking the time to send his daughter a text to be ready when he got to her uncle's house to pick her up. As he pulled out from the curb, he noticed a man in a camouflage jacket helping load the empty plastic bins into one of the vans Westen used to haul the decorations from the town's storage facility. Something about him seemed familiar, but he didn't have time to get a good look at the man, Saturday shoppers honked at him to vacate the parking spot. He obliged and focused on the afternoon's task at hand.

Chapter Seven

Monty paused with the pitchfork in her hands as the truck pulled into the parking area near the barn. She tossed the load of hay into the wheelbarrow and set the fork safely against the wall so no one would trip on it and get injured. Removing her work gloves, she walked outside to greet Callie as she climbed out of the cab and ran around the front of the truck, while her dad went towards the back.

"We made cookies for the school bake sale on Monday and I brought you some," the young teen said holding out a decorated round cookie tin, a shopping bag in the other.

"Oh, you should sell those," she said, not taking them.

"Aunt Holly said we had plenty. We could all take two tins home. Dad and I have one. I thought you could share this with Mr. Bruce and Camden." Callie thrust the tin forward and this time Monty took it with a smile.

"I'll do just that and thank you."

Callie beamed and held up the shopping bag. "I also brought some apples for Sugarplum and the other horses, if that's okay?"

"Of course, but only as a rare treat. Too many can give them colic," Monty said watching Noel pull a toolbox and something that looked like a spotlight on a stand out of the back of his truck.

"What's colic?" Callie asked.

"Colic is severe abdominal pain and can be caused by very serious problems or something as simple as too many apples in their diet," she said deciding to give the teen the simplest explanation for the medical problem, then led them into the barn. "That's why we only give them as an occasional treat."

"Can they die from it?" Callie's eyes had already teared up thinking about it.

Monty didn't believe in sugar-coating things, not even to a young girl. "Sometimes, if they aren't treated."

"Then maybe I shouldn't give it to her," Callie said, her voice a little shaky.

Monty gently smiled at her. The young teen's concern for Sugarplum reassured her she'd do well helping at the farm. She'd already witnessed her enthusiasm about the horses and her friendliness towards Beth. "One apple isn't going to cause Sugarplum any problems. I promise. She's in the paddock outside. Stay on this side of the fence and wait for me. I'll come show you how to give her the apple, but I want to talk to your dad first, okay?"

Callie clutched the grocery bag in one hand and shoved the other in her coat pocket as she headed back out of the barn.

"She was very excited about coming back out today and bringing treats for everyone, especially Sugarplum," Noel said watching his daughter. "Thanks for warning her about the apples. The last thing she'd want to do is harm a horse, not the way she obsesses over them."

"I can tell. I hope it didn't sound too harsh, but if she's going to be here, she needs to know we take both our clients' and animals' welfare very seriously."

He shook his head, turning back to her. "It didn't sound harsh at all. She's old enough to know the seriousness of life. I've tried, with Nick and Holly's help, to raise her to understand that actions and decisions have consequences. Also, responsibility, not just for herself, but for others. So, it's good for her to hear it from you too."

Her cheeks heated from his approval. *Damn*, she hated being a redhead. A woman her age had no reason to blush at compliments from a man. She nodded at his hands. "I see you came equipped with your toolbox today," Monty quickly said, changing the topic.

*
**

Noel watched her cheeks redden, wondering why his words had caused Monty embarrassment. He'd meant what he said about Callie. As she entered her teen years, it was imperative she learn that every decision she made had consequences and that she had the responsibility to protect those more vulnerable than her, even a horse powerful enough to hurt her or others.

He gave her a little shrug. "The fuse box should be a fairly easy fix. I have a new one in the truck, along with a spool of wire. I should be able to get it done today."

"Are you sure? It will be dark in a little while."

"That's why I brought a battery-powered work light. Like I said, that's not a big job, and shouldn't take long, but I will have to turn off the power while I work. Even with daylight I'll need to see what I'm doing. Hopefully, I'll have the power back on before dark so I'll be able to inspect the rest of the wiring and some of the outlets. That should give me an idea of the scope of the rest of the project, the cost and how long it will take. Needless to say, the power in the barn will have to be off again while I do the rewiring if it's needed."

"Will it be safe to have the kids and horses back in the barn with just the fuse box fixed?" she asked, nibbling on her bottom lip.

"I'd love to tell you yes," he said, cushioning his words with a calm voice. He didn't want to lie to her and promise something that might be dangerous. He also didn't like to see her worry about her business, especially if it was unnecessary.

"But?"

He hesitated a moment. "Let me get the fuse box switched and the inspection done. Then we'll know how to proceed."

"Fair enough. I should let you get on with your work." She started to walk away, then paused. "Since it's almost dinner time already, would you and Callie like to stay and eat?"

He glanced up at her as he set up the portable work light. "I thought you said you couldn't cook?"

"I said I didn't bake. And I believe I told you I knew how to grill a steak," she said with a dare-to-challenge-me look. He liked that she shook off her worry, even for just a little bit, and felt comfortable enough with him to flirt.

"Steak, huh?"

"Ribeyes and baked potatoes, maybe even a salad."

"Then we accept."

"The salad sealed the deal, didn't it?"

He grinned at her. "Lady, you had me at steak."

Her laughter rang out as she strode out of the barn. Despite her determined gait, the gentle sway of her hips held his attention longer than it should.

Shaking his head, he forced himself to focus on the job at hand. The sexy redhead was way too distracting. During his time in the military and his work as an electrician he'd learned one thing. Distractions were a dangerous thing.

Chapter Eight

"What's the word, Cleetus?" Jason asked as his fellow deputy stopped into the sheriff's office.

"Just going to change into my Santa costume for the dinner at the nursing home tonight," Cleetus said, shucking out of his insulated sheriff's jacket. "I have to pick up Sylvie at the Dye Right as soon as I'm changed."

Curious, Jason hit print on the state's alert about an uptake on bank robberies in small towns this year and followed his friend down the hall inside one of the two holding cells held over from when the office was originally built. A new jail with more cells and modern security was now part of the county courthouse, so these cells were used for emergencies or for someone like Earl, one of the local homeless people, to spend a night inside out of the cold. Today it was going to be Cleetus' changing room.

"Why aren't you both changing at home?" he asked stopping before the door as his friend started unbuttoning his deputy shirt.

"We don't want Sunshine to see us in the costumes until Christmas morning."

Sunshine was the couple's daughter. Jason thought her name was fitting, not only was the little girl always happy and smiling, but her hair was also as bright red and spiky as her mother's. It was like she had a halo of sunshine rays.

"Uhm, she's still a baby."

"Yes, but as Sylvie says, Sunshine is really smart and who knows what she'll remember next year? And we want her to have the same magical belief in Santa as other kids."

"You do know she'll figure it out once you start talking, despite the fake beard, don't you?" Jason walked back to the main office as Cleetus continued to change. "And most of the kids in town know it's you."

"Sure. But we're going to try for a few Christmases at least," Cleetus called from the cell. "I stopped by the municipal building to help with putting the boxes for the town decorations back in storage."

"I thought Harriett was in charge of that," Jason said settling back into his office chair. "Didn't realize she needed help, or I would've gone over."

"She was in her usual drill sergeant mode and had all the volunteers hopping around like worker ants, that's for sure." He walked back into the front office as he was adjusting the big black belt in the middle of his costume with one hand, his fake beard and hat in the other. "I've just always tried to be there to get things put on the top shelves, especially the years when the volunteers are mostly ladies."

At several inches over six feet, Cleetus certainly didn't need a ladder for most things.

"I'm sure they appreciated your help."

"Met a new fella named Brody there. He said he met you yesterday."

Jason leaned back in his chair. "Yeah. He was in the Peaches 'N Cream when I went in for my break before closing time.

Seemed a little down on his luck. Bought him a slice of pie. Said he was looking for work. Not sure volunteering to decorate main street was what he needed."

"I don't know. There was free breakfast and lunch," Cleetus said, hooking the beard over his ears and tightening the band in the back beneath his hair to hold in in place, then he pulled on the white wig and finally the red hat with the white trim.

Not as round as some Santa's and without a 'belly that shook when he laughed, like a bowl full of jelly'. Cleetus' Santa was more like a large, well-toned, jolly giant. Jason remembered when he first appeared at the school for their Christmas party when he was a kid. Even though he knew it was Cleetus, he truly brought the spirit of the holiday with him.

"What do you know of this Brody guy?"

Jason shrugged. "Not a lot. Said he was in the military since high school. Wasn't afraid of hard work."

"Said the same thing to me. I told him to talk to Nick Fisher. He's always looking for extra manpower."

"Saw Nick's brother putting up the streetlights and decorations today. Do you think he's back in town for good?"

Cleetus finished buttoning his coat at the collar beneath the beard. "You never know. He gets called out when his special skills are needed. Good thing Nick and Holly are always here for Callie when he has to go."

"Yeah, she's a good kid."

"And a good singer. One of the highlights of the Jubilee play is when she sings O Holy Night."

"And hits that high note? Gives me chills every time," Jason said.

"Holly said Callie will be doing the song again this year." Cleetus stopped at the office door and held it open as Raleigh Henderson wheeled his chair inside.

"Hey there, Santa!" the new evening shift office manager and dispatcher said with a grin.

"Hey there, Raleigh," Cleetus replied with his own grin. "Would love to sit and chew the fat a bit, but I have to go pick up my elf and head over to the Senior Citizens holiday dinner."

"His elf?" Raleigh lifted a brow as he passed Jason's desk.

"Sylvie. They're quite the pair of holiday spirits in Westen."

Raleigh was new to town, relatively speaking. He and his wife Lara moved their family to town when she was offered the job as one of the unit managers—what most people used to call a head nurse—at the new hospital last spring. Raleigh had been a police officer in Columbus and knew the sheriff when Gage worked undercover for the drug unit back then. Injured in a bust gone bad, Raleigh ended up a paraplegic. Since the town was growing and more law enforcement was needed, Gage had approached him to take on the evening shift at the sheriff's office. He said having someone with Raleigh's law enforcement background brought another level of expertise, experience, and common sense to the department.

"Makes sense," Raleigh said pulling off his coat and sliding into his specially designed desk. "Sylvie looks like an elf everyday anyways."

"It's her size and spiky red hair," Jason said with a grin. He shoved away from his desk and pocketed his cell phone. "I'm going to go make my rounds, then stop over at the Peaches 'N Cream for dinner. You want anything?"

"Not tonight. Lara made me an early dinner and sent me with a thermos of her secret hot cocoa mix, so I'm good."

Jason snagged his jacket and baseball hat from the coat pegs by the door.

"If Earl shows up, you want him in the back cell?" Raleigh asked.

"I doubt he'll do more than stop in for a chat tonight. I saw him talking to Pastor Miller this afternoon when I was checking out all the lights going up before I came into work."

"Yeah, I saw all of them too. The town really goes out for the holidays."

"Oh, you haven't seen anything yet." Jason grinned at him. "But we won't be seeing Earl in here at night for a while, probably not until spring."

"Why not?"

"For the past few years the Baptist church gives Earl a room at night and pays for his breakfast and dinner in exchange for him keeping the sidewalks clear of snow and ice. The older he gets the more he needs to be in out of the elements. I'm pretty sure that's what the pastor was talking to him about since the weather is supposed to get colder tonight. I'll be back in about an hour. Call me if you need me."

Stepping out onto the sidewalk and inhaling the cold winter air, Jason had to admit he envied Raleigh. It must be nice to have a woman who cared about him enough to cook him a good meal and treat him to something special on a cold winter night like tonight. Trouble was, living in a small town didn't have him meeting many women his age he hadn't already grown up with and knew all their problems. Not one to wallow in self-pity, he pressed the button on the cruiser key fob to unlock the door, then climbed inside. Who knows? Westen was a growing town. Perhaps someone new in town would spark his interest.

For the past five years stranger things had happened in Westen.

Chapter Nine

"You were right," Noel said, setting his fork on his empty plate and reaching for the glass of water. "That was one of the best steaks I've ever had."

"Thank you. Like I said, I don't bake or cook, but I can handle a steak on the grill," Monty said, enjoying the satisfied look on his face.

Bruce let out a laugh. "I'd say so. You spend time on a Texas ranch, you're bound to pick up some tips on how to grill a steak." He leaned closer to Noel with a grin behind that white moustache that always forecasted some joke at her expense. "She makes a mean brisket when the mood hits her."

"She does?" Noel replied, giving her a questioning look. "And what puts her in the mood for that?"

"Large parties," Monty said. "It takes hours to make, and I helped man the smoker before holidays on the ranch. Sanchez was the main chef for the ranch, and he taught me all he knew about west Texas barbequed brisket. We'd make about ten or more depending on the size of the party."

"How long does it take to make one?" Callie asked.

"We'd put them on the night before and cook them low and

slow all night, taking turns to keep the fire going and make sure it didn't get too hot." She shoved her chair back and reached for her and Bruce's plate. "Callie, why don't you help me carry these to the sink and we'll grab that tin of cookies you brought for desert."

"Okay," the young teen said, quickly hopping up to help. "I really liked helping feed the horses today. I didn't know you scattered hay in various spots for them."

"I enjoyed your company while we worked. You take the cookie tin in while I rinse these. And don't let Bruce eat all the chocolate chip ones," Monty said from the kitchen loud enough for the two men to hear as she took the plates from Callie.

"I heard that!" her foreman called back with a chuckle.

Shaking her head, she quickly rinsed the plates and set them in the dishwasher. She might never have been much use in the kitchen before meals, but she'd become an expert at cleaning up afterwards. *"If you're not going to help cook the meal, you'd best be of good use after you've eaten."* Her mother's words were not a suggestion.

She grabbed the pot from the coffee maker and went to refill the adults' cups. "Which kind is your favorite?" she asked Callie once she was seated. Inside the tin there were four different kinds of cookies, each divided into separate plastic bags.

"The chocolate mint ones," Callie said pointing to the ones that looked like they had some sort of icing on top. "Those are my mom's recipe."

"Then that's what I'll have," she opened the bag took out one, then passed the tin to Callie, who took the same. Noel did too and Monty noticed the tenderness in his face as he took the tin from his daughter. She'd seen her father look at her mother, brothers and her like that. A man who loved his family.

Pulling her attention away, she took a bite of the cookie. "Oh wow! That's good. The mint is in the icing, right?"

Callie grinned and nodded, then swallowed her mouthful. "You put one of those green and chocolate mints on them as soon as they come out of the oven and let them melt from the heat. Aunt Holly used the back of a little spoon, but I used a toothpick to swirl them around to the edges the way Mom always did."

"You should do it that way to keep her memory fresh when you make these. What other kinds of cookies do we have?"

Callie leaned closer and started pointing at the different bags. "Coconut jam thumbprints, because Uncle Nick likes those. Date pinwheels, for Dad," she said throwing a grin his way. "Some lemon bars, because Aunt Holly says they're a tradition in her family. And chocolate chip with red and green candies for Gabriel."

"And me," Bruce said, reaching for that bag.

"How long were you in Texas?" Noel asked after taking a drink of his coffee.

"What makes you think I wasn't born there?" Monty asked, leaning back to nibble on the date swirl cookie.

"Although you have picked up a little Texas drawl, it's not enough to make you a native, like Bruce."

Bruce chuckled and reached for another cookie. "She don't even say fixin' to."

"Daaaddd," Callie whined, dropping into the slumped posture of an embarrassed teenager. She turned to Monty. "He does this all the time."

"Guesses where people come from based on their accent?"

"Yes."

"I think it's pretty impressive." She leaned towards the teen and whispered, "But he didn't guess where I'm really from yet."

That challenge seemed to brighten Callie's mood and she sat straighter. "Yeah, Dad. You haven't said where Monty's really from."

A knowing look slowly slipped over Noel's features. "If I had to guess, I'd say the Midwest."

"You're gonna have to get closer than that," Monty said a bit smugly.

He leaned back in his chair, the arrogance a little more subdued as he studied her. "When you were little what was your favorite color to draw with?"

She blinked. "You think knowing my favorite cranz going to tell you where I'm from?"

"No. But the word crayons does."

"Cranz?"

He nodded and now Callie and Bruce were looking at her funny.

"What?"

"Say that word agin," Bruce said.

"Cranz."

"I can't tell you the exact town, but I'd say you were raised somewhere in western Pennsylvania," Noel said, that quirky, half smile on his face one more.

"You got that from the way I say cranz?" She thought about the word and then it dawned on her. "Cray-ons."

"Yep. You might not have an accent like in the deep south or a Texas drawl, but certain words can give you away too. Southwestern Pennsylvania tends to put syllables together, like cranz instead of crayon."

"I see." Then she grinned. "You're right. I was born on a farm south of Pittsburgh. It's where I fell in love with horses. Then I went to college at Pitt where I became a horse trainer and therapist. I realized I needed more training, so I went to Texas to do an internship at an equestrian therapy ranch. Then this ranch was on the market and I decided to move closer to home."

"So, you came to Ohio bringing Sugarplum, Bruce and a

killer recipe for brisket with you?" Noel teased and they all laughed.

After they cleaned up the table, Bruce headed out to his room in the bunk house and Callie curled up on the couch to watch a training video on horse grooming while Noel and Monty sat at the table with his tablet open in front of them to discuss what he'd found in the barn.

"Here's the cost for today's work. The new breaker panel and the wiring I replaced. Between dinner and Callie's riding lesson tomorrow afternoon, I'd call it even."

She wanted to argue with him, but just looking at the numbers on the screen made her anxious, so she'd take his word for that. It was an even trade. "Okay. I'm good with that. Now what did you find for the rest of the barn? And more importantly how much is it going to cost me?"

"The good news is I didn't find anymore areas where the mice were snacking on the wire casings. So the imminent danger of a fire breaking out has been dealt with today with the work I did."

He paused and she inhaled, hearing the silent "but" in that pause.

"And the bad news?"

"You and Bruce were right. Nothing has been updated since the facility was built nearly seventy years ago. It all needs to be brought up to code, the wiring in the barn replaced and incased in metal conduit to prevent the little vermin from destroying it again. For safety sake."

The weight of that information settled on her shoulders. "And how much is that going to cost me?"

"The cost of wire, conduit, new outlets—based on the prices at the Knobs & Knockers," he looked at her, "I presume you'd like to buy local instead of big box store?"

"Of course."

"It's going to run you around a thousand dollars."

"And the labor?" She fixed him with a steady gaze. "And don't for a moment tell me you'll do that for free."

"I wouldn't insult you like that and Nick would have my head, since it's his business I represent, but I can do a twenty-five present discount. I'll need to bring out another worker to get the work done quickly so you're not losing more therapy hours than necessary. Depending on how many hours that takes, I'd charge another thousand dollars on the labor."

She rested her elbow on the table and pressed her mouth against her knuckles as she considered the state of her bank account, the monies owed, Bruce and Camden's salaries, and her monthly bills. Swallowing hard, she stared at the fire in her fireplace as fought back the tears that threatened to form in her eyes. She wasn't a wishy-washy emotional woman. This was her business and she needed to figure this problem out.

Noel's warm hand settled on her free hand on the table, drawing her attention back to him. "Is this going to break your business?"

"I've been able to break even the past few months, but this winter was going to be tight, due to the weather. I hadn't planned on a two-thousand dollar surprise expense."

He squeezed her hand then released it. "You could talk to Beth's father."

"Beth? My client you met yesterday?"

Noel nodded. "Yep."

She shook her head. "I can't ask a client's parent to loan me the money."

"No, but you can ask the manager of the bank, whose daughter is delighting in the benefits she receives from your therapy business, for a line of credit."

Chapter Ten

"You're sure this is the bank we want to hit?" Karl asked for the third time. "Couldn't we go somewhere warmer? Like Florida?"

Kurt twisted his neck from side to side, waiting for that delicious pop that kept him from backhanding his brother in the mouth. Karl wasn't the brightest bulb in the pack, probably because by the time their mom was carrying him, she was deep into coke then descended quickly into crack. She'd barely survived that, making a recovery to sobriety for a few years only to succumb to opioids ten years ago, leaving him the responsibility as a teen to provide and care for Karl. It's why they were a two-man team. He wouldn't trust anyone else to treat his brother right.

"I told you before, this town's bank is special. They get deliveries from the state every four months to dole out to the community because some Meth dealer tried to blow up half the town and the DEA and state DOJ knew about it and didn't try to stop it."

"I like all the Christmas decorations. Maybe we could dress up like Santa when we rob them," Karl laughed, changing topics like a motorcycle on the interstate being chased by cops. Sometimes it was like working with a dog chasing squirrels.

"Focus Karl. Remember we're not hitting this bank like all the others."

"Yeah, because they had cameras. I made sure my face mask was in place."

"Yes. You did. The problem was you were supposed to wear the plain black hoodie. Not the one with the Steelers' logo on the back."

"I'm hungry. Can we get burgers?"

And off he went on another trail. Sometimes he just wanted to leave him on the side of the road somewhere and move on with his life. But he wouldn't. He'd promised his mom.

"We will in a bit," he said, focusing his binoculars on the door of the café as it opened. Out walked two guys who looked like truckers.

"Fries and a chocolate shake too?"

"If you stop asking questions."

"Okay."

Silence reigned in the car for the next two minutes. A near record for Karl.

"Why don't we just go in and get them now?"

He sighed. "I told you."

"We have to do it so no one knows it's us. We do it when there are lots of people around."

"That's right. We do it when they have their festival."

"Yuletide Jubilee," Karl corrected him pointing to the poster on the window of the dress shop they were parked next to in the alley.

Across the street a sheriff's deputy walked up to the door of the café. He opened it and held it as a family exited. A father, mother and three kids. Kurt focused his binoculars on the family and followed them to their car. He wanted them to be on their way before he and Karl went to get dinner in the diner. He wanted their faces to be unfamiliar to them. It's why he and his brother were wearing blue hoodies, black shirts and jeans. No logos this time. Anonymous.

The sedan pulled out of the café parking lot driving west towards the older part of town. He set the binoculars on the floor beneath him, "Okay, let's get something to eat."

"Yes!" Karl fist-pumped and climbed out the passenger side.

They stopped at the sidewalk just as a truck pulled up outside the sheriff's office on the katy-corner side of the street. Kurt blinked, not really trusting his eyesight at the passengers climbing out.

"Look it's Santa and an elf," Karl said, pointing towards the truck.

"Don't point." Kurt grabbed his brother's arm and steered him towards the café. This was the weirdest little town, but the payoff was going to be massive if his plan worked out.

Chapter Eleven

"You know, I think I've solved your problem on how to contribute to the Jubilee," Noel said later Sunday afternoon as he watched Callie ride Sugarplum around the outdoor paddock area with Bruce holding the lead.

Monty shifted her gaze from his daughter to him as they leaned against the fencing. "By giving horse-rides?"

"Now that you mention it, you could put in a series of free lessons in the silent auction. Great way to get some PR during the festival," he said wondering why he hadn't thought to suggest that to her before.

"There's a silent auction?"

"It starts on Friday at the Jubilee market. There's usually specially made craft items like a quilt, a free weekend stay at one of the vacation cabins in the area, dinner gift cards at the cafés and the other restaurants in town. Stuff like that. Then the winners are announced after the final performance of the play on Sunday evening."

"What do the auction proceeds go to?"

He looked back to see Callie safely on the far side of the paddock with Bruce, no longer looking scared so high up on the horse. Seeing how secure she was, he leaned one arm onto the top of the fence as he turned to face Monty. "All the proceeds from the auction, the play, and the Saturday's dinner goes to the Yuletide Jubilee fund as it always has since the very first Jubilee back during the Depression. The proprietors of the craft booths at the market donate a minimum of their earnings to the fund as well. Then the town council donates the money to various causes, like the sports teams of the middle and high schools, as well as the bands for equipment and instruments. They help people in need like supplying the homeless shelter and the Westen House for teens in need. Sometimes it goes to specific families."

"Then I'll definitely donate free lessons for the auction. Good idea."

"It is, but that's not what I meant by contributing."

She quirked her head to the side to study him curiously. "What did you mean?"

"I was thinking about the Saturday dinner and dance."

"How can I contribute to that? I don't really dance."

"No, but according to you and Bruce, you do cook a real mean Texas brisket."

Her face lit up as she realized what he meant. "You think I could cook a brisket for the dinner? What a good idea. How many people usually come?"

"Last year they sold out their tickets at three hundred. Rumor is they're hoping for five hundred."

"Oh. That's a lot of brisket." Her previous joy was replaced by instant disappointment.

"All the meats for the burgers and brats the Peaches 'N Cream cooks for the dinner is donated by Mike Hough from the Chop Shop butcher shop. He gets the PR and he gets a tax deduction to charity. How many briskets do you think you'd need for that big of a dinner?"

"I've cooked for a hundred twice before and usually had about fifty pounds of brisket. That means I'd need about two hundred and fifty pounds for that many people, *if* we want a pound of brisket per person."

"I don't think kids are going to eat a pound of brisket, no matter how good it is and like I said, there will be burgers, hot dogs and brats, along with side dishes and desserts."

"In that case we could cook half that amount. Say a hundred and twenty-five pounds?"

"How long would it take you to cook that much meat?"

"When I made it for the last holiday party before I moved here, fifty pounds was four briskets and took fifteen hours to smoke and cook. I can probably fit six in the smoker I have, but that's only going to give us half the amount we'd need. So, I'd have to cook two batches."

"Can you do that?"

She smiled. "Brisket is easy to reheat once it's gone through the initial smoking and cooking phase. If I start on Thursday, by Saturday morning it should all be done and easy to transport to town for the dinner with a quick reheat there."

He pulled out his phone and flipped through his contacts, then hit dial.

"Who are you calling?"

He held up his hand as the phone connected. "Hey, Mike! Good to see you at church this morning. Yes, Callie and Deliah's duet on *What Child Is This?* was great. Your daughter certainly knows how to harmonize." He paused with a wink at Monty to listen to the butcher wax on about his daughter and how the girls' voices really blended together. "I couldn't agree more. Hey, I have a question for you. How long would it take you to get a hundred and twenty five pounds of brisket for the Jubilee's Saturday night dinner?"

"Thursday morning?" he glanced at Monty, who nodded.

"That would be great." He paused again. "Sure. I'll talk to Lorna about adding it to the menu and Mayor Maggie about the cost of the food donation from you. See you Thursday."

He hung up and pocketed the phone.

"Why did you do that?" she asked, not looking overly thankful he'd just taken care of the brisket problem for her.

"Mike's daughter and Callie are friends and choir mates. We've known each other awhile. It was an easy call and he's glad to do it."

"I didn't say I could do it. I have a business to run."

"One which is going to have to close down for at least a day for the wiring repair to take place."

"Which I can't afford right now."

"And you can't afford to wait. I can come by and work on Thursday and Friday, you can spend the time doing the brisket and then pay the invoice to Nick's company when you have the money."

"And your brother's going to be okay with this?"

He shrugged. "He will be once I tell him the plan."

She shook her head, staring at him with a half-exasperated, half-amused look on her face. "Do you always get your way?"

"Yes," he said, not even trying to hide his smile. "I'm a Captain in the Army, a partner in Nick's business, and a father of one."

"You're a bit arrogant too."

He laughed. "Confidence and competence aren't arrogance." He leaned closer, all humor gone. "But, you're right. I shouldn't have ordered the meat without your permission and commitment."

"No, you shouldn't have. I'm not your daughter, your employee or one of your soldiers." Then she took a deep breath and slowly exhaled. "But I do want to help with the Jubilee somehow."

"Then you'll do it?" he asked, just as Bruce brought Callie and Buttercup to a stop in front of them.

"Do what?" the foreman asked.

Monty glanced Noel's way, then back at the other two. "I'm making brisket for the Saturday night dinner."

**

"That was a great meal, Holly," Noel said, leaning back in his seat.

Even before Holly and Nick were married, Sunday dinners were a family tradition at her, now their, home. Today it was roasted chicken, dressing, gravy, and roasted veggies. With their mother in a nursing home in Florida, this was a way for them to stay connected as a family, besides just for holidays and birthdays. Of course, with Callie spending weeks at a time with her aunt and uncle while he was deployed on missions, the family's dynamics had tightened. Holly served as a surrogate mother figure in his daughter's life, something he'd be eternally grateful for.

"Thank you," she said with a grin, seated with her feet up on another chair and her hand on her very pregnant tummy while her husband cleared the table. "I'm sure it isn't nearly as good as the steaks you had yesterday."

"How did you know about the steaks?" He paused as he heard his daughter and nephew giggling from where they were playing in the family room. "Callie."

"Don't be mad. While we were setting the table, she was telling me about being at the ranch yesterday to help with the horses and you working on the wiring in the barn, then having dinner with Monty and her foreman. That was after she gushed on about getting to ride a horse for the first time."

"That was this afternoon." He remembered the grin on his

daughter's face when she finished riding Sugarplum. "She really enjoyed that. And I have to say, she took as much interest in grooming the mare afterward."

"So, you're going to let her take riding lessons? Isn't that a little costly?" she asked as her husband set a glass of water in front of her, to which she made a scrunched up face.

Noel tried not to laugh. It was a known fact that his sister-in-law preferred anything to drinking water, but her doctor, and now her husband, insisted she drink eight eight-ounce glasses of water minimum in a day during her pregnancy.

"He's got a barter system to help pay for Callie's lessons," Nick said sitting by his wife.

"Oh?" Holly said, raising both her eyebrows his direction, and Noel wanted to punch his brother for bringing it up. He settled for casting him a scowl instead.

"The fuse box for the barn and training facility needed replacing. It was a very quick fix."

"And while he was at it, he inspected the entire facility and discovered nothing had been updated since it was built back in nineteen-fifty something," his brother said.

"Really?" Holly asked.

"Yes." Noel reached for his glass of tea and took a sip. "Monty said the farm was vacant since the previous owner died."

"Mr. Carstairs," Holly said.

"His two daughters took a while to get it sold and so rats got into the barn. They decided nibbling on the casement of the old wires was a good snack. Which was the problem at the old fuse box. I replaced it with new wiring and an actual breaker panel, both designed to keep the rodent problem under control. Along with the cats she's got out there now."

"So, fixing the fuse box problem was your trade for Callie's riding lessons?"

"Not exactly."

Nick chuckled. "Nope. He's going to rewire the entire facility and barn, encasing it all in metal conduit to be sure to discourage the rats from having midnight snacks. At cost."

"At cost?" Holly swung her gaze to her husband. "What does that mean?"

"It's not going to be just at cost," Noel said, drawing her attention back to him and trying not to lose his temper with his younger brother. "It will be the cost of the supplies—wiring, conduit, outlet boxes—and any extra labor needed to get the job done in a day, two at the most."

"Extra labor?" Holly asked.

Nick grinned. "He's not adding the cost of *his* labor to the invoice, just his helpers' hours."

"I see," Holly said with a grin.

"It's not like that," he started to protest. "Monty needs a safe facility for her animals and her clients, one of which will be my daughter. I happen to have the skill and time to see it gets done properly."

"And getting free riding lessons for Callie while spending time with the hot therapist doesn't have anything to do with his altruistic offer," Nick said with a laugh.

Holly stared at him. "You think my friend is *hot*?"

Noel tried to hide his grin as his brother had just stepped into a pile of manure.

"Whoa, honey." Nick held his hands up in mock surrender. "You know you're the only woman for me. I was just saying that Noel might consider—"

"Her hot?"

"I was teasing my brother when I said that. I do not think your friend is hot." Nick laid his hand over her belly and stared deeply into her eyes. "Monty isn't on my radar. No one but you are. You know how beautiful I think you are while

72

bringing me my own little girl into this world? To me that's sexy as hell."

He leaned forward to kiss her.

Noel shifted his gaze to where Callie and Gabriel were playing. One of the things he envied his brother was having a loving wife in his life. It had been four years and he still missed Rebecca. She'd been his whole world and the damn cancer had stolen her from him and his daughter much too soon.

If he was honest, he'd been pretty much numb since her death. His focus solely on providing for Callie and making sure she was taken care of—physically, securely and emotionally. His brother wasn't wrong. Meeting Monty the other day had been like touching a live wire. For the first time in years, he'd been interested in a woman. It wasn't just her looks. She was smart. Strong. Independent. Vibrant.

He liked spending time with her, listening to her voice as she talked about her horses and how they helped her clients in therapy. She genuinely liked spending time with Callie—he'd witnessed that throughout dinner on Saturday and again on Sunday when she was teaching her how to groom Sugarplum.

It also felt good being needed by a woman again. Not that she needed him because she wasn't capable of handling things. Running her own therapy practice and managing her ranch proved how capable she was. He couldn't teach horse riding, hadn't been on one himself in years. He knew nothing about therapy. Bringing her facility up to safety code? That was something he had a specific skill set for that she didn't. And he'd never admit it out loud in this day and age, but his male ego liked knowing she had a need he could fulfill.

"So when is this rewiring project going to start?" Holly asked, drawing his attention.

"Thursday. The power to the barn will need to be off while I work, so Monty is rescheduling her therapy sessions."

"Oh no, that's going to drive her crazy," Holly said with a little laugh, then added for the bemused look he and his brother gave her. "Monty hates not being busy."

"Oh, she'll be busy," Callie said, coming over to get two iced cookie-cutter cookies in the shape of Christmas trees. "She's going to be smoking brisket for the Saturday night Jubilee dinner."

"Really?" his sister-in-law said.

"Yep," she said handing one of the cookies to her little cousin. "Dad talked her into doing it today at the ranch."

"Really?" Holly said again, this time exchanging a knowing look with his brother.

Noel shook his head at the pair. "Apparently, according to Bruce, her foreman, she cooks a mean Texas brisket. She's been looking for some way to contribute to the Jubilee and I suggested she do that. Since it will take two days to smoke that much meat, I suggested I rewire the barn on those days so she wouldn't be losing extra therapy hours to get both projects done. Simple organizational planning."

"Something he learned in the Army," Nick said.

"I was always organized."

"Not according to mom. She said our room was like walking into the local dump."

"No," he said. "She said your room was like walking into a dump. Mine was like walking into an antique store."

"An antique store?" Holly asked.

"He had junk all over the place," Nick teased.

"Not junk. Collections. And unlike you, I kept them in orderly piles."

"Like in an antique store," Holly said with a grin, then she paused. "Your house doesn't look anything like that now."

"That was the Army's influence," Nick said.

"And Rebecca's," Noel said. "She hated clutter. When we

74

were first married, she told me I had to start culling my collections. Gave me a limit of two."

"Two?" Holly looked incredulous at the idea. She waved her hand around her kitchen. "I have three just in here. My cookie jars." She pointed to the rack by the door that contained ceramic cookie jars from different decades. "Then there's the cookbooks," she said pointing to the shelf near her pantry. "And of course, my two Blue Ridge pottery patterns." One of which was presently holding the Christmas cookies she'd served up as dessert.

"Well, Rebecca would've considered the last two as necessary, since you use them regularly. My tools weren't part of the culling process for her. I ended up keeping my baseball collectibles, including baseball trading cards and—"

"The *Star Wars* character models!" Holly said. "I love seeing all of them in your glass case."

"Which Rebecca insisted I get or get rid of my *little action figures* as she called them." Noel smiled at the memory. The wall clock chimed nine. He stood. "Okay, that's my reminder to get Callie home. There's still one more week of school before Christmas break and she needs to get in bed. She's a bear to wake up in the morning if she doesn't get enough sleep."

"I am not," his daughter said, putting on her coat as she walked up to them.

"Yes, you are," all three adults answered.

She rolled her eyes. "I guess I can't argue with all' of you."

Hugs were given all around. Noel and Callie headed out the door just as the snow started falling in big fat flakes.

"Snow!" Gabriel yelled from his father's arms.

"Oh, maybe school will be cancelled tomorrow!" Callie said just as excited.

"Don't get your hopes up, kiddo," Noel said as they headed for the truck. "It's only calling for a few inches tonight."

"A girl can pray," she said as she buckled herself into her seat. "Pastor Miller's sermon was on the Bible verse Matthew seven seven today. 'Ask and it shall be given to you; seek and you shall find; knock and it shall be opened unto you.' So, I'm asking."

He shook his head as he pulled out onto the street. "I'm pretty sure that's not what the pastor or the scripture was meant for."

She shrugged. "Well, that's what I'm asking for. A snow day."

He knew he should lecture her more, but frankly was just glad that she'd listened to the sermon and knew the Bible verse. Who knew how far into her teens she'd continue to carry that faith? And maybe not getting a snow day would teach her that even when you ask for things, sometimes, like when he'd prayed for Rebecca's healing, the answer is no.

Chapter Twelve

"Thank you so much, Mr. Watters," Monty said as the bank's loan officer walked her to the exit on Wednesday. The snowfall Sunday night and into Monday morning had indeed been more than a few inches and kept her busy at the farm the past two days. Now she had time to meet with the banker about her electrical upgrades. "I appreciate you not only helping me secure the line of credit, but explaining to me how it works."

"Jay, please. My daughter Beth just loves her therapy sessions with you. It's not only in your and the bank's best interest that the property is properly updated to safety standards, but our family's too," the tall slender bank manager said and opened the door for her.

"And I do love having Beth come for her sessions with us. She and Sugarplum are becoming quite good friends." She stepped outside and he followed her out.

"Will you be at the Jubilee this weekend?"

"Yes. I'm smoking brisket for the dinner."

"Brisket?"

"Supposedly, she's an expert at Texas brisket," a familiar deep voice sounded behind her.

She turned to see Noel standing behind her.

"I am. Trust me."

He grinned at her. "I'll be the judge of that."

"Hey, Noel. Good to see you," Jay said, shaking hands. "The street decorations look fantastic."

"Thanks. I had lots of help. Now I just have to pray that everything goes well at the tree lighting ceremony on Friday night."

"I'm sure it will. Talked to Henry and Mags over at the Petal Pushers yesterday and they said they have the kissing bough all decorated and ready to hoist in the gazebo after the tree lighting ceremony."

"Great. I'll stop by there and double check the measurements to be sure it fits."

"I'm pretty sure it will. Henry and Mags have been providing that bough for years. See you Friday then," Jay said and stepped back into the warmth of his bank.

"So, where are you heading?"

"Over to the Chop Shop to pick up the brisket. Mike said he had it ready and I don't want to take up too much of his meat locker with it. What are you doing here?"

"I was headed over to the Knobs & Knockers to pick up the rest of the material for your job and saw your truck parked outside the bank. How did it go?" he asked.

"Good. He set me up with a generous line of credit. More than I really need and I can access it as I need to upgrade the farm over the next few years. The key will be to pay it back after each project, so no big payment at the end will put the farm or the business in jeopardy."

"I see you had a long talk with Jay. He had the same talk with Nick when he started the construction company. Jay may be a banker, but he wants the people in this town to succeed and not to get in over their heads with debt."

"I like him. You can tell how much he loves his daughter too."

"Have you eaten lunch yet?" he asked.

"No, I haven't."

"Want to grab something over at the Peaches 'N Cream? The Wednesday special is chicken and dumplings," he said with a half grin and a wiggle of his eyebrows."

"Let me guess. One of your favorites?"

"Almost as good as my mama's," he said, taking her elbow and escorting her across the street.

"Where does your mother live?" she asked as they fell into step down the sidewalk towards the café.

"After our dad died, she moved from Columbus to Clearwater, Florida. Said she wasn't going to spend another cold-to-her-bones winter up North. She'd come spend the summer with us the first few years."

"Oh. Not anymore?"

He shook his head and reached for the café door. "No. She just turned seventy-five, but her arthritis is limiting her ability to care for herself, so she's moved into an extended care home for seniors down there. She's in the selfcare part of the facility, but it also has a medical unit, so she can go there for physical therapy and treatment as needed. Callie and I visited her last spring. It's a pretty nice place and she's made friends. Booth or table?"

"Booth?"

He nodded and followed her over. After they shucked the coats and scooted into their seats, they gave their orders to the waitress Glenna for chicken and dumplings. The whole café had taken on a festive holiday mood with big colored Christmas lights reminiscent of the ones from the nineteen-forties or fifties outlining each of the windows. Holiday wreaths also hung suspended in front of those windows, while holiday music played from the vintage jukebox.

"So, I have a question," Monty said.

"Shoot."

"What is the kissing bough?"

He grinned at her. "I asked the same question the first year we lived here."

"And?"

"It's a tradition here in Westen. Every year, a huge ball of mistletoe is made and decorated with ribbons and lights, then hung in the gazebo," he said as Glenna returned with their food. "It's sort of a legend here."

"Oh, it's the most romantic thing," Glenna said with a wistful look on her face. "The legend goes like this. If you love someone, you must kiss them beneath the bough before Christmas Eve, and you'll marry them in the next year."

"What happens if you don't?" she asked.

"Oh, that's the dreadful part. If you don't, you'll lose their love forever."

"Really?" she looked from one to the other, and they both nodded with grave solemnity. "I've never heard of this legend before."

"It's been around since Isaiah MacNab settled on the outskirts of town back in the early nineteen hundreds. It was a tradition in his family back in Scotland, and the town adopted it." Noel said.

"Especially after he had a party, and four couples who kissed under the bough, including Isaiah and his girlfriend Hannah, all married within the next year," Glenna added.

"And it's been true time after time over the years," Lorna said, stopping at their table. "We raise the kissing bough to hang in the gazebo right after the Christmas tree is lit. You wouldn't believe the number of couples who hurry to get their kiss in so as not to fulfill the other part of the legend."

"The part where you lose them forever?" Monty asked, quite intrigued by the story.

Lorna leaned one hip against Noel's side of the booth as Glenna went to serve another customer. "The legend goes that at that same Christmas party Isaiah threw a couple who were engaged to marry the next spring didn't kiss under his kissing bough that night or any time before Christmas Eve. Sadly, the groom-to-be fell ill and died before they could marry. So, they must've not been true loves or soulmates."

"That just meant they weren't in love, Lorna, not jinxed by some old legend," Noel said.

"Okay. During World War II, Violet and Nola Miller were both dating young men who left to fight in the war right after Pearl Harbor happened. Neither couple got to kiss under the bough because it hadn't been raised before the men left for the army. While both men lived, neither came back to Westen for either of the twins." Lorna fixed him with a don't-tell-me-it's-not-true look, then strolled on to the next booth.

"I guess she told you," Monty said and they both chuckled as they dug into their lunch.

"Callie really enjoys helping with the horses," he said halfway through his meal.

After the heavy snow Sunday night that did indeed make for a half-snow day for the kids, he and Callie had arrived with a snowplow attached to his truck. He explained that even though Andre Thornton, the assistant county roads commissioner had his crews keeping the main roads cleared, the drive from the road to the barn and house at her place wouldn't get plowed. While he cleared her drive and helped Bruce shovel the side-walks—the foreman complaining about how cold it already was compared to December in Texas. Noel informing him this was just the beginning and they would have more snow than this if the Almanac was correct—Callie had helped Monty spread feed for the horses.

"She's a good helper and I enjoy her company while we work."

"The horses really like the treats she gives them, that's for sure," he paused to drink some coffee.

"We give them carrots a couple of times a week for the vitamins in them. Letting her feed them helps her bond with them, not be afraid of the animal and lets the horses know she's there to care for them."

"What about that black Stallion in the back corral area? Why do you keep him separated from the others? I noticed you don't let Callie feed him, just you or Bruce."

Finished with her meal, she set her fork and knife on the plate and used her napkin. "Percy is a rescue."

"What do you mean rescue?" he asked, laying his napkin on the table and pushing his plate slightly forward.

"One day I was traveling from the ranch where I worked delivering a pair of mares to another ranch. On the way back, I stopped at a little dive place for a bite to eat. Barbecue of course."

He grinned. "Of course."

"I decided to take it down the road to a shady spot and enjoy a little picnic of sorts. That spot happened to be across this little country road from a dilapidated farm, overrun with weeds. Sitting there, eating a really good pulled pork sandwich, I saw something move on that farm. I crossed over the gravel road and looked over the barbed wire fence—which I personally think is barbaric, by the way."

"I think I'd agree with that, but we don't see much of it up her in Westen."

"So, looking closer, I saw this black stallion chained to the side of a barn. Even from where I was, I could see his ribs. I had to do something."

"Tell me you didn't go in there by yourself," he said with a look she hadn't seen since her father found her sitting in the principal's office for fighting. The bully had deserved the black eye and busted lip. But her father wouldn't listen to her side of the story until she was home, suspended for a week. A week in which she'd had to learn that while her anger was understood, her courage appreciated and applauded, but her decision to take it on herself instead of going to someone in authority pointed out as her ultimate error in judgement.

"No," she said with a bit of mockery in her voice. "I first took pictures with my phone, then I drove into town and met with the sheriff. As soon as he saw my pictures, he went out to check on the animal along with someone from their county animal control people.

"Turns out the former owner of the farm had just abandoned it and the horse, leaving him to slowly starve to death."

"That's horrible."

"The good news is that I offered to take him for no cost, which would save the county the cost of feed, board and medical care. The bad news was that he'd been so mistreated, it took every trick I knew just to get him in the horse trailer. Restoring his physical health had been way easier than his mental health. He tolerates me and Bruce, but his trust of others? I don't dare let him near the other horses or any clients, yet. It's like he has PTSD."

"Do you think he'll ever overcome it?"

"With time and patience. Maybe. I think it's going to depend on what kind of outcome I expect for him. If I want him to be a therapy horse? I don't see that happening. He'll trust us to feed him, to care for him, but I haven't seen him connect with me or Bruce in any way that says he'd trust us to break him to a saddle much less ride him or have a client interact with him. Safety—for him and us—is the most important part of inter-acting with him. If I just expect him to thrive and live a free life in the back corral? That is already achieved, although I'd be sorry there wasn't more for him."

"Then I'm glad you're keeping him away from the others, especially since my daughter is helping with the horses. I know it's impossible for me to protect her from every possible threat, but knowing you've got limits for her regarding a horse like him," he paused and stared out the window a moment. "Let's just say it eases some worry for me. And I've learned to take all the help I can get with raising her."

"It must be hard being a single parent."

He huffed a deep breath and shook his head. "You have no idea."

"When did you lose your wife?" she asked even though Holly had already told her.

"Five years ago. Although she'd been sick for nearly two years before then. The final year, when it became apparent that neither chemo or radiation was going to kick its butt, I took a medical leave from the Army until after she passed. Nick moved here to help care for Callie if my unit got called up and that's when he met Holly. Thankfully, they've been her extended family since I've been called away six times since then. Some-times for a week, sometimes a few months."

"It must be hard to be away from her, even for something as important as missions with the Army."

"It is. When Rebecca entered fourth stage, I intended to take a hardship discharge, but she wouldn't hear of it."

"Oh? Why not?"

"When we met, she was with the International Red Cross. My unit was in Iraq, working with them to provide relief and health services to local villages. She was helping set up schools for girls."

"You worked as the interpreter for them?" she asked, then hurried on when he gave her a quizzical look. "Holly told me you speak several languages."

"A few more than several," he said with a little lift to the corner of his mouth.

She tried not to return it no matter how much she liked the little show of male arrogance. For a moment he seemed perfect —the caring father, the loving husband who cared for his dying wife, the man who interpreted for a compassionate relief organization helping girls get an education in a nation that didn't cherish them before the war or afterwards. His arrogance about his language skills put a small chink in that perfection. And she'd never liked perfection.

"How many?"

"Well, English."

"No, really?" she said with sarcasm.

That little grin got bigger. "French, Spanish, Portuguese, German, Russian, Kurdish, Arabic in several dialects, and a little Chinese."

"Wow." She sat back in her seat. "Why only a little Chinese?"

The grin left and he toyed with his coffee mug. "A personal decision not to learn too much."

She considered those words and understanding hit her. "Because you don't want them to call you away more than they already do."

He nodded. "Every time I leave Callie, even for a weekend the guilt gets worse. Given the state of the world these days, I'm choosing to put her and my family before the country this time."

"Do you want to know what I think?" she said.

"Can I stop you?"

"No. Despite what you think, you don't have anything to feel guilty about. Callie is loved and she knows it."

He gave a derisive laugh. "Sometimes I wonder when she gives me sarcasm or sass."

"That's how you know she knows. She's comfortable testing you because she's secure in knowing you, your brother and Holly love her. She knows you hate being gone, but you've made her a safe space with her aunt and uncle. And while you want to give into her desires, you do so with limits. She can learn to ride, but she has to do the work at the farm to help care for the horses." She reached across the table to lay her hand on his. "You're doing the right things. And I don't think anyone really wants you to learn more Chinese, not anyone who is really important."

"You ready for dessert?" Glenna said coming back to the table.

Monty quickly pulled her hand back and looked at her watch. "Uhm, no, I need to get going."

"I'll take the check," Noel said, and held up his hand when she started to protest. "It's my treat this time."

"Thank you."

After paying the bill, he walked with her back to her truck.

"I'll follow you over to the Chop Shop and help load up those briskets," he said as she opened the driver's door.

"You don't have to do that."

"Least I can do, since I conned you into cooking them."

"Yes, you did." She pressed her lips together and studied the sky a moment, making him think she was considering his offer. "Okay. I'll take the help."

Chapter Thirteen

"Hello Ms. Taylor. Hey there, Noel!" Mike Hough called out from behind the glass enclosed case in the center of the butcher shop. "What can I do for you?"

The inside of the Chop Shop looked like one of those old fashioned butcher shops you saw in the delis of New York in old movies, complete with the black and white checkered floors like the Peaches 'N Cream Café had. Different cuts of meat and poultry were on display in the right side of the glass case. The smaller left side held the deli meats and cheeses. And three standup glass cases held prepackaged meats, poultry and some spreads like ham salad or dips.

Customers milled about, the Miller twins were discussing whether they should order a crown roast this year or do another turkey. Mike's wife Carrie helped a young mother with a baby in a stroller and one on her hip at the cash register. A man in a beat up camouflage jacket and knitted skull cap seemed to be studying the deli selections. Noel had seen him the day before helping Harriett pack up the Christmas decorations boxes after they'd been emptied by the other volunteers.

"I'm here to help Ms. Taylor pick up those briskets for the Jubilee dinner," Noel said, pulling his attention away from the other man. "Did they come in?"

"Sure thing. Thankfully, Andre had the main roads good to go after Sunday's storm, so the delivery truck had no problem getting through. Awful early to be getting snowed in."

"Does that happen often here?" Monty asked. "Getting snowed in?"

Mike washed his hands and dried them. "It's different each year. Some years it's not more than a few inches like on Sunday. Others, half the northern part of the state gets socked in like we did about five years ago. Power went off to half the county and people were snowed in for days, especially out in the more rural parts. Andre and his crew did manage to get the main roads and highway cleaned in just a day or two. But heavy snows like that are usually much later in winter. Your meat's in the back I had to get it delivered from several of the local meat processing plants since we put in the order so late and on little notice. But they were happy to help."

"Local meat processors?" Monty asked.

"My family has always believed in buying and selling locally grown and processed meats. None of this buying from big companies who are owned by foreign countries. We're in Ohio, we should support Ohio businesses and farms."

He went into the back and returned with two plastic bins piled high with wrapped packages and set them on the ground, exhaling heavily at the effort. "Got to say, that's an awful lot of brisket."

Monty squatted down and pulled out one of the brown paper packages to read the label. "Are they all about the same size?"

"Pretty much within a half-pound more or less," Mike said. "Let me get you a receipt."

Monty shot Noel a panicked look. He understood immediately. He'd told her the cost of the meat for the supper was covered by the Yuletide Jubilee committee's fund.

"Don't forget the committee is paying for the meat, Mike," he said.

"Oh, I know. I made several copies. One for me, one for the committee and one for Ms. Taylor. Tax deduction purposes for me. Records for the committee. And I thought Ms. Taylor might need one too. It lists each brisket by weight and where we purchased it from." He handed Monty the ribbon of receipt paper. "You should have this for taxes, so you can write off the cost of smoking the briskets."

She gave him a surprised look. "Oh, good idea."

Mike's brother Jack stuck his head out from the back room. "Delivery, Mike. They need your signature."

The butcher looked at the two tubs of meat.

"You got ahead, Mike," Noel said. "I've got this."

"You sure?" the big man hesitated

Noel glanced to his side at the man still staring at the deli meats. "Brody?" he called hoping he'd gotten the name right.

The man turned. "Yeah?"

"Mind giving me a hand here?"

He shrugged and walked over. "Sure."

"Great. We're just loading them in the silver truck outside."

Monty grabbed the door for them as they each hefted one of the bins and headed outside.

"Thank you both," Monty said once they were loaded.

"You're welcome, ma'am," Brody said and headed back into the shop.

Noel studied him a moment.

"Do you know him?" she asked.

"No. He's new in town. He helped out with hanging the lighting last week. Seems like a loner."

"Well it was nice of him to help load the meat," she said, climbing into the driver's seat. "I think Bruce and I can manage getting them into the house at the farm."

"Dismissing my help already?" he teased.

"No. I do appreciate it. But didn't you tell me you needed to get materials for my electrical repair job today?" she said with a teasing smile of her own.

"You are correct."

"Then be on your way. I have a hundred and twenty-five pounds of meat to rub down."

"Now that sound like fun."

Her cheeks heated immediately when she realized what she'd said. "You know what I meant."

Laughing, he stepped away so she could close her door. She waved before pulling out onto Main Street. He watched her turn at the light before looking back into the butcher shop and the man once again contemplating the cut meats.

His decision made, he opened the door.

Brody stared at the ham and turkey in the meat case. The shop offered sandwiches and if he ordered right, he'd have enough money in his pocket to pay for three lunches. He'd hoped to find some work off the books as a handy man or gopher in this small place, but all the people seemed to be volunteering instead of working for pay. The short older lady, Harriett had commandeered him into helping last week—he hadn't dared say no. She reminded him of his old drill sergeant from boot camp in the way she gave orders—and insisted he take the hundred dollars at the end of the day. His pride had him almost refusing, but she'd stuck the folded wad of bills in his coat pocket and told him not to be a fool.

He hadn't. He'd used it to get a hot meal that night. He'd found an alley off one of the side streets and spent the night in his car, something he'd gotten used to in the past year as he traveled around. But even only having one meal a day now, the money had dwindled to almost nothing, especially since he'd had to run the engine on Sunday night not to freeze to death when the snow came pouring down.

"Made your decision yet?"

He looked to the left to see the man named Noel standing beside him again.

"Ham and swiss looks good."

"I'm a turkey and American on sourdough man myself," the other man said. "I was wondering if you were busy this afternoon?"

"Not particularly. Why?" he said, hoping he wasn't being volunteered for another chore. He didn't mind helping out, but he really needed to find some way of making enough money for a room over at the boarding house. Another night in the cold sounded miserable, even for someone used to outdoor living over the years.

"I'm needing some help uploading material for a job I'm doing tomorrow and Friday. I'd gladly buy you lunch if you'd give me a hand."

Brody nodded. His mother hadn't raised a fool. "I can do that."

"Okay," Noel said and waved the butcher's wife over. "We'll take two ham and swiss on—" He looked at him for the answer.

"Sourdough with mustard would be good," Brody answered.

Noel nodded. "And two turkey and American on sourdough with mustard, Carrie. And we'll take them to go. Thanks."

"Anything to drink?" she asked as she pulled out the ham to slice up.

"We'll get some waters," Noel answered.

Brody went to the tall glass cabinet stocked with sodas and water, grabbing two.

Noel took one of the waters and handed Brody the bag of sandwiches as they walked out to his truck. "You go ahead and eat while we head over to the Knobs & Knockers."

"This town and their shop names." Brody shook his head with a slight grin.

Noel chuckled. "Yeah, it's like they're trying to see who can be the most unique. But you get used to it. Makes the whole town a bit different from other small towns."

"I've noticed." The man tucked into one of the ham sandwiches like he hadn't had a good meal in a few days.

Noel drove down Main Street while his passenger ate, wondering what had brought the man to Westen. These days there were lots of newcomers in town. Many brought in by the residential development and new jobs created since the near catastrophic explosion on the outskirts of town years ago. The friendliness of the old time Westen residents attracted those searching for something more than the metropolitan areas offered—a sense of belonging or a sense of purpose. Which one had drawn Brody here?

"Been traveling around the area long?" he asked as he stopped at the red light at the corner where the Knobs & Knockers sat.

Brody swallowed the last of the sandwich he'd nearly inhaled and then drank some water before answering. "For a while."

Okay. Brody's a man who treats words like gold.

Noel turned right and then pulled into the store's side parking lot. "Looking for any particular kind of work?"

"Not afraid of manual labor."

"Know anything about electrical work?" Noel asked putting the truck in park.

"Know you should turn off the power before touching anything electrical."

"Rule number one." Noel agreed with a bit of humor. "The reason I'm asking is I have a project out at Ms. Taylor's horse farm that's a four-day job for a single electrician. The work time could be cut in half with a second person helping. My brother and I have a construction company and I could take one of our regular workers to help me, but then that slows down the other projects we already have going. Standard pay for out laborers starts at twenty-two dollars per hour. Depending on how many hours it takes us, you could earn between three-fifty and four-fifty working today and tomorrow."

"Cash?"

Something in the way he asked that caught Noel's attention. "Before I agree to that, I need to ask you some questions."

"Fair enough."

"Are you wanted in any illegal matter or are there warrants out for you arrest?"

"No, sir. Neither." Brody met him eye-to-eye when he answered, without blinking and without hesitation.

"Is there a reason you want to be paid only in cash?"

"I'm simply wanting to be off the grid for a while. I gave sixteen years to the government to guarantee other people's freedom. Thought I'd enjoy some of my own, is all."

Again, Noel couldn't read any deception in the man's face, voice or words. A skill he'd honed to a sharp edge as an interpreter. "Then you've got a job for the next two days, well three, since I'm going to put you to work right now." He held out his hand and Brody shook it. Noel's father taught him and Nick that you could tell a lot about a person by their handshake. Brody's was good, strong and suggested dependability.

If he guessed, he'd think Brody was hiding from something,

he just prayed he hadn't misjudged his character based on his gut and a handshake.

Chapter Fourteen

"What's going on?" Bobby Justice asked her husband as Gage came in the back door, a worried look on his face.

As the town sheriff, he often wore that expression. It could be something as simple as cows had blocked the main highway again—although she doubted that was the case tonight because of the cold snowy weather this time of year—or a major crime had been committed. He walked to the tall cupboard and opened the gun safe they had mounted inside, out of reach of their children, removed his gun from his holster and secured it inside.

"Daddy!" Their four-year old son Luke ran across the room to get scooped up into his father's arms for a hug, which relaxed her husband's expression, so she knew whatever was wrong wasn't an imminent problem or emergency.

"Hey buddy. Have you been a good boy for your mommy today?" Gage asked, switching the preschooler into his right arm then leaning down to kiss Bobby as she stirred the pot of soup on the stove. "Mmm, potato soup. What else you got?"

"Some fresh focaccia bread from the Yeast & West bakery,

where I also picked up a cranberry pie for dessert. Although this would be enough for Luke and me," she said picking up the potholders, she opened the oven and pulled out a casserole dish of grilled beer brats covered in sour kraut, "just for you, some meat."

He grinned at her. "Sounds like a great meal. Where's Blythe?"

"Poor baby is cutting teeth and was cranky as could be. I fed her early, gave her a bath and put her to bed. Hopefully, she won't have a bad night. You two go wash up and we'll eat." She paused and fixed Gage with a stare. "Then you can tell me what's bothering you."

"You know me too well," he said and carried Luke off to the downstairs powder room.

They were working on their pie and ice cream when she breached the subject again.

"So, what has you worried tonight?"

Gage set his fork on his empty plate and reached for his coffee. "You read that bulletin about the bank robbery team?"

"The one that came out last week?" she asked as she wiped her son's mouth and hands with a wet wipe. "Yes. Something new happen? Did they rob another bank?"

He leaned back in his chair, that concerned expression back on his handsome face. "No. And that's what has me worried."

"Why?"

"They've been hitting banks in small towns all over north-eastern Ohio in a circle around Westen. They've hit one every other week like clockwork. It's been three weeks."

"And you think we're next." It wasn't a question. Almost from the day they'd met she'd been able to read his mind, sort of connect the dots between his non-verbal communication and the words he wasn't saying. She continued to follow that path he'd started down. "And with the Yuletide Jubilee happening this weekend, we're sitting ducks for them?"

"If not this weekend, with all the vendors at the Jubilee, the play ticket sales, all the stores expecting record shoppers, then definitely on Monday when the bank takes in cash proceeds from the Jubilee."

She'd read the statewide alert memos. "So far they haven't been violent."

"No, but that doesn't mean they aren't dangerous." He drained the last of his water and scooped up Luke as he climbed out of his chair. He nuzzled the little boy's neck, making him giggle.

Bobby relaxed as she watched the pair.

A former undercover narcotics cop, Gage had always been intense. Loyal to his family, friends and his town. The man would put his life on the line for any of them. Becoming a father added to that responsibility probably ten-fold, but it also touched something inside him she didn't think even she could reach. Both Luke and Blythe eased something inside him. Spending time with them seemed to lighten his moods, brought him joy. Oh, he was still intense and would destroy anyone or anything that threatened to harm either child, of that she had no doubt and oddly it gave her comfort for their safety. It was the love for their children that had driven the darkness he'd seen in mankind into the deepest recesses of his soul and she thanked God every day for that. She also thanked God for giving this man and her children for her to love.

"You give Luke his bath and tuck him in, tonight," she said picking up the dirty dishes and heading for the sink. "Then you can tell me all about your security plans for the weekend over a drink."

"I like the way you think, Deputy," he said as he shifted his son under one arm like a large wiggly football, stopping to give her a heated, but brief kiss, then sauntered out of the room like a man who had the world at his feet.

As she cleaned up the kitchen and set the coffee maker ready for the morning, she reflected on how much her life had changed in the past nearly six years. Back then she'd lived in a big city among thousands of people, yet felt all alone. Her work as a teacher, while fulfilling in helping her students, left her disgruntled and wishing for more. And at over thirty-five, she'd given up on ever finding the love of her life or having a family of her own.

Now she lived in a small town, where she knew many of the people, and more importantly they cared about her as much as she did them. She'd changed careers by becoming one of the sheriff deputies, which gave her a chance to still help people. Not only did she have the love of her life in Gage, but she was so proud of the work he did as Sheriff and one of the town's leaders. And of course there were her two children. They weren't perfect little angels. They were their father's children too, but she wouldn't trade a moment of this life to go back to things the way they'd been before. Empty and sad.

If Gage was worried about trouble coming to their town, she was concerned too. He wasn't the only one who would lay down their life to protect the ones they loved—hadn't she done it six years before to crawl in that hole after him? They were a team. God help anyone who threatened their town or their family.

Chapter Fifteen

"How much chili powder did you order?" Bruce asked as he carried the box in from the front porch. He set it down on the kitchen table and looked at the slabs of brisket Monty had already unwrapped.

She looked up from the piece she was trimming the fat from to grin at him. "It's not just chili powder. There's onion powder, garlic, cumin, smoked paprika and brown sugar. Enough to marinate a hundred and twenty-five pounds of meat for the next twelve hours."

"Good thing the only thing you have in that fridge is condiments and salad greens."

"There's burgers and steaks in the freezer. You don't starve working here," she said, setting the knife on the cutting board and putting the brisket in the plastic container with the others she'd already trimmed. After washing her hands, she reached into the cupboard for her largest glass mixing bowl.

"You're right, I ain't starvin'. But I sure do miss fried chicken and chili, not to mention some of Miz Juanita's cornbread," Bruce said, opening the box and pulling out large containers of the spices Monty had ordered online.

She laid her hands flat on the butcher-block countertop and stared him straight in the eye. "I miss her and her cooking too, but after what happened at the Cross-Corner ranch I wasn't ever setting foot on it again. You could've stayed on if you wanted."

"I know. I'm not saying I made a mistake by leaving. Hell, I couldn't stomach what happened, either. It's why I left with you. Just missin' me some homemade cornbread." He held up the big bag of salt. "You think you got enough of this or are we makin' a salt lick for the horses?"

Salt licks were a way for horses to get not only the salt they needed for electrolyte balance in their diet, some also contained minerals they also needed. She hung several in the barn and the outside corral for her animals.

"You know as well as I do that one bag isn't going to be enough to make even one salt lick," she said with a laugh and was glad he'd changed the subject.

For four years she'd worked at the Cross-Corner ranch in north central Texas as one of their three equestrian therapists then the owner died. A former corporate CEO, Grant Barret had been a good man, a protector of those who'd come to the ranch for therapy. He'd started the equestrian program with his wife, Teresa before she was diagnosed with cancer and kept it going after she died as a promise to her. They had one son, Tony, whom Monty met on the day of his father's funeral.

Pompous, arrogant, and self-righteous were the nicest things she could say about the man. He'd come home long enough to hear the will being read and immediately informed all the staff that he was closing the therapy program in order to change the ranch over to a dude ranch and hunting business. Juanita was offered a position to remain as cook for the new enterprise, as well as some of the ranch hands, including Bruce, but the therapists were given one month's severance pay and a swift don't-let-the-door-hit-you-on-the-way-out send off.

Wanting to be closer to her brothers who now had children, Monty had already been looking at properties in the Midwest to begin her own therapy program. She'd contacted the realty agent for her new home and quickly finalized the purchase. Once that was done it was easy for her to pack up her belongings and Sugarplum, whom she'd bought from Grant the year before, and the still healing Percy. And that's when it happened.

"What the hell do you think you're doing?" Tony yelled as he stormed across the drive to the barn where she was loading up Sugarplum.

"What does it look like I'm doing," she said, not trying to keep the sarcasm out of her voice as she led the mare by her reins towards the loading ramp, where Percy already nervously waited in his side of the two-horse trailer.

He grabbed the reins and shoved her aside. "It looks like you're stealing property of the Cross-Corner."

"Hey! That's my horse, you ass!" She lunged for the reins.

He turned to one side and backhanded her.

Suddenly, she saw stars as she staggered back. The taste of iron in her mouth. Damn that hurt.

"Try to take these horses or that trailer and I'll make you hurt worse. No one steals from Tony Barret."

"How about someone shooting little Tony Barret," Bruce said.

Monty and Tony both swung around to find the cowboy aiming his shotgun straight at the man's chest.

"I suggest you let loose of those reins and step away from Miz Montgomery. Or I'm going to shoot you. We respect our women in these parts, boy." He waved the gun slightly, indicating the man should move to the right and away from Monty and her horse.

Tony had enough sense to let go of the reins and moved in the direction he indicated. "You'll both go to jail. Those horses and trailer are property of the Cross-Corner."

"Miz. Montgomery, you want to fill him in?" Bruce asked without moving his rifle aim from Tony.

She swiped away the blood from her cut lip and chin with the back of her hand, then reached into her back jeans pocket, pulling out the papers she'd slipped in there just for such a confrontation, although she hadn't thought it would get physical.

"These are the bills of sale for both the horse trailer, the mare named Sugarplum, and the stallion named Percy. They're all dated last year."

"How do I know they're not forgeries?"

Bruce took a step forward at the other man's menacing tone. The fool really didn't know when to close his mouth.

"You can take my word for it, or read your father's signature, or check with the county clerk. It was all done legally, with witnesses. Seems your father didn't trust you." She led her horse up the trailer and secured her, then turned to Bruce.

"You still coming?"

"Yes, ma'am. Just as soon as you're on the road, I'll be right behind you."

"You're leaving too?" Tony asked, sounding all blustery still.

Monty hadn't waited to hear what Bruce had to say to him. She'd climbed into her truck and headed off the ranch, then turned Northeast towards Ohio.

"What time you wantin' to start the smokin' of these beauties?" Bruce asked, pulling her back to the present.

She picked up the large spoon and paused to calculate the timetable for the next day. "There's a little over a hundred and twenty-five pounds of meat, and I've only done fifty pounds at a time. I don't want to overload it or the meat won't cook thoroughly. I guess we'll need three batches in the smoker at a time and about twelve hours for each one. I guess we better start the fire in the smoker about six."

"Good thing I got extra firewood while you was out galivantin' around with your electrician."

She shook her head as she worked on mixing the spice rub. "We weren't galivanting around and Noel is not *my* electrician."

"The man's an electrician, right?"

"Yes."

"You hired him to fix your electrical problem, right?"

"Yes."

"Then he's your electrician," Bruce said with a wink over his shoulder. "I don't know what you were thinkin' about."

She laughed. And she did know exactly what he'd meant. Funny thing was, she sort of liked thinking of Noel Fisher as her own personal electrician. She certainly felt a tingling of excitement and a spark of heat when he was around.

"You know, he's a good man, your electrician," Bruce said as he got another plastic tub out of the pantry. "Works with his hands for his brother's company, raisin' Callie by hisself, still protectin' the country."

"You're making him sound like a saint. Does he walk on water too?" she teased.

Bruce turned and stared at her with those cool blue eyes of his, all his usual humor gone. "All I'm sayin' is he ain't like that Tony. You can trust him."

"I agree." Scooping out the rub, she liberally sprinkled it over the slabs of meat in the tub. She set aside the scoop and washed her hands before beginning to rub the spices all over each slab of meat, covering them on both sides. "What I don't understand, is when did you become a matchmaker?"

"Well, someone has to do it. Ain't seen you meetin' up with anyone since we came to town."

"I've been busy."

"Looks more like you've been hidin' out here. A young woman like yourself should be attractin' men like bees to honeysuckle."

She snorted out a laugh as she worked. "Now you've gone from matchmaker to poet. I guess I should be honored you didn't compare me to a carcass attracting flies."

He set down his trimming knife, washed his hands and turned to look at her with both hands on his hips, obviously in lecture mode—a stance she'd seen from both him and her father more than once. "When you first came to the Cross-Corner, I thought you'd be causin' all kinds of trouble with men circlin' you, but you brushed everyone of them off. Sort of made me think you might be preferring girls. That thought fizzled quickly, when I saw you at one of the horse shows. I could see you eyeing some of the cowboys, but sort of slid into the shadows if any of them came our way. Now, talkin' about horses? Talkin' about your therapy programs? You can talk all day. So, I quickly figured out you were shy with the young whippersnappers. But it's time you got over that. It ain't right for a woman like you to be alone."

"I'm not alone."

"Me. Rufus and your horses don't count. Besides, I ain't gonna be around forever. You need a man and a family. And I just think it's time you get on with findin' one."

Finished, he turned and headed for the door.

"Where are you going now?"

"Time to check on the horses. You can handle this brisket makin' all on your own."

"Surprised you don't think I need a husband for that too," she muttered.

"I heard that," he yelled into the house as he shut the door behind him.

She heaved a sigh. She ought to be furious with Bruce for

sticking his nose into her personal love life, or lack thereof. Many women lived happy, productive lives without being married or even having children. Trouble was, she'd always wanted both those things. She'd also been extremely shy as a child and into her teens.

When other girls were learning how to talk and flirt with boys as teenagers, she'd been more interested in her horses. In fact, working with horses helped her overcome her shyness, at least when it came to talking about horses with others. Discovering how much working and learning about horses eased her own anxiety in talking with others, she'd pursued her career as a therapist. It also gave her confidence when bringing on new clients, allowing her to give reassurance to parents and family members that this type of therapy would indeed be beneficial and might surprise them on how their loved ones would respond to the horses.

Talking and flirting with men?

She sighed again, washed her hands and covered the first bin of briskets with plastic wrap before placing them in the refrigerator and starting the rub process on the second tub.

Talking to men in any way other than in a business situation still intimidated her. She still was amazed that she'd stood up to Tony that last day at the Cross-Corner. If she'd only been defending herself, she probably wouldn't have done it. But his threat to take Sugarplum and Percy from her? Her inner courage shot right to the top. Still, she'd never learned to flirt with men, to put herself forward for their attention. Mostly, being around men in social situations intimidated her. Which was weird, because her father hadn't. Neither had her brothers. But they were family, not strangers.

Except for Noel.

The morning they met, she'd been relaxed from holding onto Sugarplum and chatting with both Callie and Holly, so he hadn't seemed so intimidating, even when he stepped between her, Sugarplum and the swarm of excited teens. She had to admit she'd appreciated having a his help herding those kids in. She hadn't had to ask. Noel hadn't moved aside to watch what would happen. No, he'd assessed the situation and took charge. Not because she couldn't manage the kids on her own, but because the safety of her, Sugarplum and all the kids was at risk by the sudden surge of teenage bodies. His quick reaction left her the freedom to secure and reassure her horse.

Since then, she'd grown more and more comfortable talking with him. Noel was genuinely interested in her equestrian therapy program. Then the question of safety when it came to his daughter and the electrical situation of her barn facility only heightened his interest. He hadn't just informed her there was an issue with the wiring. No, he'd just simply taken charge of fixing it and giving her a plan to take care of paying for it.

Noel reminded her of her father. See a problem, fix it. Don't wait for others to take the initiative, get a hammer and nails, or come up with a solution plan and implement it.

She liked that. She liked him. He was easy for her to talk to, even though he was very handsome. She just hoped her awareness of him as a man wouldn't make her nervous around him while he was here tomorrow working.

Tap. Tap. Tap.

Brody jumped at the wrapping against the passenger side window, his hand going to his hip before he realized he wasn't armed.

Years of habit. Hard to shake.

Looking out the window he saw the little older lady he'd

met helping decorate the streetlights. *What was her name? Harriett.*

She motioned at the door and he pushed the unlock button.

Cold air rushed in when she opened the door. He expected her to climb inside. Instead she shoved a sleeping bag at him.

"If you're going to sleep out here, don't freeze to death. We don't have time for dead bodies this weekend." She handed him a thermos. "Hot chocolate."

"You're not calling the sheriff on me?" he asked taking the thermos. The heat of it warmed his hands.

"Other than freezing to death, you planning anything else stupid tonight?"

The little woman didn't pull any punches with her words.

"No, ma'am."

"Then I won't be informing the law on one condition."

He hesitated. There was a catch. In all his years in the military and growing up in foster homes, he'd learned one thing. Nothing was ever free. If someone did something nice for you, there was always a cost.

"What's the condition?"

"You come to the clinic first thing in the morning to talk with Doc Clint."

He thrust the thermos back her direction. "Can't do it."

"Can't or won't?" she asked, peering in at him in the car's dim overhead light.

"Can't. Have to go to work."

"Work where?"

"Electrician guy, Noel Fisher wants me to help with a job. Have to meet him at the café at eight."

She thrust the thermos back his way. "Good. You be at the clinic at seven to see the doc. And bring back my thermos."

"He has office hours that early?" he asked, surprised. Most

doctors he'd been to see since coming back to the states all seemed to start their hours at nine or later.

"He will tomorrow."

Before Brody could ask her any more questions or thank her for the sleeping bag and hot chocolate, she slammed the door shut and disappeared down the alley.

Shaking his head, he opened the thermos and poured himself some of the delicious smelling liquid. He'd driven into town, his old sedan on fumes and stopped for dinner at the diner last week. Since then, he'd met some odd characters in this town. But no one seemed threatening. Well, maybe Harriett, but he was twice her size, so he was pretty sure he could take her if he had to.

He unfurled the sleeping bag and pulled it over his legs and body, then set the driver's seat back to stretch out a bit as he drank the chocolate.

Today hadn't been as bad as he'd thought when he'd woken up. Not only had Noel hired him to help with the electrical job tomorrow, he'd given him all four sandwiches from the butcher shop, then paid him for helping load up the electrical equipment at the hardware store. He'd decided to pocket that money for tonight, since the next night was supposed to be colder and he'd use the money plus his pay for working with Noel to get a warm room at one of the motels on the highway. Now, he had a thermal sleeping bag to make his night in the car less miserable than he'd expected.

Westen was a strange town all right. But maybe, it's a place he could stay for a while.

Chapter Sixteen

"What do you think?" Dr. Clint Preston asked his nurse as he watched Brody walk down the sidewalk in the lightly falling snow flurries towards the Peaches 'N Cream Café.

"His last name isn't Smith."

"I didn't think so either. He did say he was ex-military, but I couldn't get what branch. Claims he has no family and is just traveling the country. Not that I'm an expert, but he doesn't seem to be overtly dangerous."

"No. More like lost," she said walking away.

Clint inhaled and exhaled, then followed her. It was going to be one of those days. If he wanted any information out of his laconic nurse, he was going to have to drag it out of her syllable by syllable. "I'm a general practitioner, Harriett. Not a psychiatrist, so I'm not sure what kind of evaluation you expected me to give you."

"Didn't need one."

"You dragged me out of bed at the butt-crack of dawn, insisting I needed to meet with this man this morning. If you didn't need an evaluation of him, what the hell did you need?"

he asked, following her into the laboratory section of the clinic and staring at her incredulously.

She held up three tubes of blood. "An excuse to get blood samples."

"What for? I didn't order any."

She set the purple and green topped tubes on the counter. "Complete blood count and routine chemistry. Just to be sure there's nothing wrong with him medically."

"And the red top?"

"DNA test."

"A swab would've been easier."

"Would've spooked him."

He ran his hand through his hair and gave a nod at the thermos Brody had brought with him. "And that?"

"Fingerprints."

She reached into the cupboard under the counter and pulled out a black box. As he watched, she brought out what looked like fingerprinting tools he'd seen on crime investigation shows.

"I'd ask if you shouldn't be having Gage or one of his deputies do this, but you're not planning on telling him about this, are you?"

"No."

"Harriett?"

She paused with the fan looking brush in her hand to look at him.

"I suppose you intend to send the blood and fingerprints to someone you know, in some agency with three letters that I'm not supposed to ask you about, right?"

"Right."

"Why?"

"Quickest way to the answers."

"You realize this man is staying off the grid because he doesn't want to be found, don't you?'

She blinked and gave him that disconcerting stare she always wore when she thought you'd just asked a stupid question.

"But you think there's a reason to find out his identity, don't you?"

"Like I said, he's lost."

"So, you're going to take it upon yourself to find out his identity and what unit in the military he belongs to."

"He's a PJ."

He blinked. Once again he'd lost track of the conversation. A common occurrence with Harriett. "A what?"

"Airforce pararescue."

"And you know this how?" He was beginning to wonder if she was psychic.

"The patch on his shirt. Got a look at it the other day when he was helping us hang the Christmas lights on Main Street. Saw it again today when I drew his blood."

"Another reason you wanted him to come here, so you could confirm what you saw."

She gave him and enigmatic smile that said he was a bright boy for catching on and kept on removing the fingerprint impressions from the thermos with a long strip of special tape. At seventy, the woman's mind was still sharp as a tack. She could outthink him and was usually ten steps ahead of everyone else. Long ago he'd given up trying to fight the rumors and believed like all the locals that Harriett was once—and might still be—with the CIA.

"You know you're going to have to explain to Gage why you're running fingerprints on Brody."

She simply raised one brow his direction, then picked up an

overnight mailing envelope, slipped the tube of blood and the card with the fingerprints inside.

"And you're not going to inform the town's chief law enforcement officer of what you're up to, are you?" He shook his head already knowing his own answer. "Of course you aren't. And if my wife's cousin comes and asks me about it, what am I supposed to say to Gage?"

"He won't. Besides, I will tell him if there's any reason to involve him in this. I'm simply going to appease my own sense of curiosity, nothing more."

It was his turn to raise and eyebrow her direction. "Harriett, I've been working with you long enough, to know you do nothing simply for curiosity." He held up his hand when she started to speak. "Just promise me, you'll let me know if I need to worry about the safety of anyone from this man. Otherwise, I'm going to go have breakfast with my family...and take some aspirin for my suddenly throbbing head."

*
**

Noel pulled up outside the horse barn a little after nine. Smoke was already pouring from the big grill outside the farmhouse.

"Looks like Monty already has her briskets smoking away," Noel said as he and Brody climbed out of his truck.

"Monty is the lady we helped at the butcher shop yesterday?"

Noel nodded and pulled on his work gloves. He opened the tailgate and lifted out two of the four small square-shaped battery powered work lights. "Montgomery Taylor. She owns this farm and runs an equestrian therapy program. Let's get the lights set up first, then we'll get the tools and wires."

Brody hefted up the two remaining lights and followed him into the barn. "What is an equestrian therapy program?"

"We use horses to help people with all kinds of issues," Monty said, coming out of the back stall where the stallion had been, a shovel full of manure and hay in her hand. She dumped the contents into a tall barrel, then covered it with the lid and set the shovel to the side. Taking off her gloves, she set them in the handle of the shovel.

"Shoveling manure already this morning?" Noel said. He liked how her cheeks always colored when he teased her.

"Yes. And it's all your fault."

"How's that?"

"Since you needed all the horses out of the barn, I put Percy in the side paddock to get some exercise and fresh air for a bit. Good excuse to muck out his stall and put down fresh hay while you work in there."

"Want us to get that stall done first?" He asked as he carried the lights over near the small room where he'd replaced the circuit panel. "Just set them down here for now, Brody. This is Ms. Taylor. Monty, this is my day helper for your project, Brody Smith."

"Ma'am," he said briefly shaking the hand she offered.

"Please call me Monty, Brody," she said with a smile, which he didn't quite return.

He turned his attention to Noel instead. "Want me to get the toolbox or the generator, boss?"

"Just the toolbox. It'll take both of us to get that generator over here, but I'm hoping we won't have to use it."

"Okay," the other man said and sauntered away.

Monty gave him a curious look. "Is he always like that?"

"Don't know. He's only been in town about a week as far as I can tell."

"Is he an electrician too?"

Noel shook his head. "No. He's just a man needing some work. He seems to have a sensible head on his shoulders and if I don't have to pull one of our regulars off the jobs Nick already has going to help me, then it's a win for everyone."

"What's his story then?"

"Don't know. We had breakfast this morning. He doesn't talk too much and all I got out of him was he'd been in the military and now was out to see the country he'd fought for. I get a feeling there's something more, but it was like pulling teeth to get that much out of him."

She gave a shiver and rubbed her arms. "Mucking out the barn always makes me work up a sweat. I left my coat in there," she said nodding at the tack room behind him.

"Oh."

Realizing he was blocking the doorway, he stepped aside. It was his turn to feel embarrassed. Smiling with a bit of sass in her eyes, she brushed his body as she slipped into the room. It took major self-control not to grab her by the arms, haul her up against him and kiss her senseless.

Pulling on her green coat, she flipped out the long braid of thick red hair from beneath the collar to land in the fur line hood behind her.

Damn he wanted to run his fingers through her hair and see if it was as warm as it looked.

"Noel?"

Oh, crap, she'd asked him something. "I'm sorry, what did you ask me?"

"How far do you think you'll get today?"

Ignoring the unconscious seductive innuendo of her words, he considered her actual question. "We'll disconnect all the old sockets and light switches first. Then start wiring and adding the new socket boxes. Even though they're not outdoors, winter can cause freezing even in a sheltered space, so I went ahead and got waterproof ones that have caps on them for when they're not in use, if that's okay with you?"

"Sure. I hadn't thought of that. It would probably be a fire safety thing too, wouldn't it?"

"I'd have to check with Deke Reynolds, the fire chief about the fire code for an outdoor structure like this barn, but I'm sure these are well above the requirements." He walked to the back of the barn where she'd been cleaning out Percy's stall. The smaller paddock was right outside, and the stallion was trotting around. "Looks like he's enjoying the exercise."

"It's good to see him trotting," she said, coming to stand beside him. "When we first brought him here, he had no idea how to act like a normal horse. I tried putting him in the bigger paddock with Sugarplum, but he was skittish and backed himself into a corner whenever she came near. He also barely let me groom him the first two months. Keeping him in the stall was for his own safety, as well as everyone else's."

"What happened to him?" Brody asked, coming up on her other side.

"He was abused, malnourished and chained to the side of a barn that was half falling in on itself. We got him away from his owner and brought him here to heal."

"It takes a long time," Brody said, almost under his breath.

Monty turned a questioning look to Noel. He returned it with a shrug. The other man spoke as if he understood exactly what the horse was going through. From their talks the past two days, he'd gotten the idea that pushing him for more information about his past wouldn't be appreciated.

"We'd best get started," he said instead. "Brody, you set up two of those lights at the far end of the barn and I'll set up two here, then we'll turn the power off."

Brody nodded and they all walked back to the tack room.

"I'll get out of your way, but lunch will be ready about noon," Monty said.

"Brisket?" Noel asked as she followed Brody back to the barn entrance.

She grinned over her shoulder at him as she kept walking. "No. Those are on the smoker grill and the first batch won't be finished until six tonight. I'll have burgers from the smaller grill."

"Gotta love a woman who has two grills and knows how to use them," he muttered and hefted up the remaining lights to take to the back entrance.

*
**

Halfway through the morning, Monty grabbed an apple from the basket on the table and went outside to check the temperature on the smoker. She didn't want it too high, or the meat would char and the flavor terrible, too low and it wouldn't cook through. Satisfied that the briskets were doing well, she wandered over to the barn, curious how Noel and Brody were progressing.

She expected to see the pair hard at work, but Noel was sitting on a bale of hay drinking coffee while Brody stood in the back door watching Percy in the rear corral.

"Finished already?" she teased as she neared Noel.

With a smile he shook his head and lifted his coffee mug, the thermos sitting on the ground by his work boot. "Nope. Got all the sockets disconnected and thought we'd take a little break before we start pulling the old wiring out."

"Sounds good. Was checking on the briskets and thought I'd see how things were going." She nodded towards Brody. "How's he doing?"

Noel's attention shifted that direction. "Good. Follows directions well. Quiet though."

"No more information about how he ended up in Westen?"

"Not a bit." He glanced at the apple in her hand. "Snack for you?"

"No, Percy. He usually doesn't take them, but I thought maybe..."

"He might take them from someone who's been through trauma too. Someone like my helper?"

"It's just a hunch. I doubt Brody will volunteer for therapy, but if he thought he was helping a fellow survivor, they both benefit from the bonding."

The corner of Noel's lips lifted in a toothless smile. "Lady, you have a good heart."

And her cheeks heated once more. The man had a way of making her blush, but she was beginning to like it. She tossed the apple in the air and caught it. "Let's see if Percy can do some magic."

Brody stood leaning on the rail, watching the stallion walk around the corral. Monty approached him on the left. One of her former clients told her he always wanted his family on his left side. His wife didn't understand that he needed to keep his right hand free in case he needed to reach for a weapon when he was in the Army. Even though he was discharged and shouldn't fear an attack, he still wanted that ability, that little bit of control over any situation. Monty didn't know if Brody had that same left-over need to keep his gun hand free, but she did know he was right handed.

"He's liking this little bit of freedom," he said, nodding at Percy. "But he keeps looking at his stall."

"His safe space," she said leaning her arms on the top of the rail. "Being in his stall where he gets his food and water, where no one hurts him. It makes him feel safe."

"He should be happy he has that place."

"He was chained up for so long, he doesn't really know how to act like other horses and the one time I let him out with other horses he tried to fight them. It's taken a long time for him to trust Bruce and me, but just barely."

"I know how he feels."

Monty didn't say anymore. She just continued to watch Percy move around the far end of the little corral. Slowly, he made his way closer to them, approaching Brody's side. The quiet man didn't move, just looked straight at the horse.

Percy lifted his front leg and scratched at the ground.

Monty held her breath.

Percy shook his head.

Brody kept staring. Finally, he held out his hand, palm down.

Percy stepped forward, putting his nose under Brody's hand.

Tears filled Monty's eyes. She handed the apple toward Brody.

"What's that for?"

"It's a treat. He usually won't take them from us. I have to lay it on the floor of his stall. See if he'll take it from you."

Brody stared at it a moment then took it and turned slightly towards the horse. He kept stroking Percy's forehead while bringing the apple to his muzzle. The big stallion's nostrils wiggled as he sniffed the treat, then he drew back his lips and mouth to take the apple from Brody.

"You're good with him," Monty said after a few minutes.

"I'm not a trainer," he said.

"No. You're a friend. Believe it or not animals are like us in many ways. Forming friendships is one of them." Having sown that seed in his mind, she looked at her watch. "Time to get back to work. Thanks for getting him to take the apple. For him, it's progress."

She headed back through the barn and met Noel's gaze as she passed, giving him a little thumbs up that Brody couldn't see. Noel nodded.

"Hey Brody. Let's get going on pulling the wiring," he called out.

Monty grinned as she left the barn. She liked helping people. She liked helping animals. Getting someone in need of help to help someone else? As the commercial would say—priceless.

*
**

"You fellas want to give me a hand?" Bruce asked, after he pulled the small tractor and trailer to a stop outside the barn an hour after they'd finished lunch. He used the setup to deliver feed to the horses out in the far pasture.

Noel looked up from wiring the socket across from Percy's stall, which was next on their spot to work. They'd managed to remove all the old sockets and switch boxes, leaving them in place to mark where they needed to be replaced, pulled all the old wiring throughout the barn before lunch. Brody turned out to be a quick study and knew how to follow orders without missing a beat. Probably his military training. Now they were working on rewiring the new sockets.

"What's up?" Noel asked the older man.

"I need your help pulling something out of the old garage." The foreman turned and walked in that direction.

Curious, Noel took off his gloves, setting them and his screwdriver on top of the spool of wire where they'd been working.

"What's he up to?" Brody asked, following suit.

119

"Haven't a clue."

"Is he Monty's father?"

"Nope. He's her foreman. A real Texas cowboy."

"Looks like he's been on a horse his whole life," Brody said as they watched the other man stalk up the gravel drive past the farmhouse.

Noel nodded in agreement. Bruce walked with a bowlegged strut as if he had just climbed off a horse he'd been riding for two days. He wondered if his gait was from years in the saddle, arthritis, rickets, or a combination of all three.

"We've been so busy gettin' this place up and runnin' for Monty, I ain't had time to check out all the other buildings. I was fixin' to get around to it a bit sooner than this," Bruce said when they stopped outside the building that looked more like an old barn than a garage. It also looked like it was built prior to the barn and farmhouse.

"How old is this garage?" Noel asked.

"Don't rightly know. Might've been a barn from near the turn of the century before the farmland here abouts was sold off in parcels."

"Looks like it's gonna collapse in the next big windstorm," Brody muttered.

Bruce chuckled. "It do, don't it?"

"You sure you should be messing around in there?" Noel asked, looking skeptically at the nearly collapsing roof.

"Probably not. Been puttin' it off for a while, but since y'all were going to have the barn off limits, thought I'd see what was in here. And I found this." He went to one of the two doors and pulled it open, then opened the other.

Inside sat something draped in an old painter's tarp. Bruce pulled it off and discharged a ton of dust covering it to reveal a red, old fashioned, two-bench, horse-drawn sleigh.

"Wow," Brody said.

"Does Monty know this is here?" Noel asked as they ventured inside to look it over.

"Not yet. Found it yesterday while she was in town pickin' up those briskets. Thought I'd pull it out and see what kinda condition it's in first. Is it worth cleanin' up and use this winter or do we just get it hauled off to the scrap heap?"

"Let's get it out of there before the roof comes crashing down on it then."

Bruce picked up a thick rope he'd laid outside the garage and went to the front of the sleigh. Looping it around the bar stretching across the front, he tied it off expertly. "I figure you two could lift and shove from the sides while I pull from the middle."

"You sure you don't want one of us to do the pulling?" Noel asked.

The older man shook his head. "Been handling bulls that're heavier than this thing all my life. You just give it some movement and we'll get'er out there."

Noel exchanged a what-the-heck look with Brody and they took up their positions on either side of the sleigh.

"We'll go on three," Bruce said, looping the other end of the rope around his body. Grasping hold of it over one shoulder, he turned his back to them and started counting.

On three Noel gave a slight lift to the sleigh and shoved forward. Brody matched his movements and with surprising ease, the sleigh slid out of the garage. They kept moving it until it slid over the gravel driveway and up onto the bank of snow-covered grass beyond.

"Whew-ee," Bruce crowed with enthusiasm as he came around from the front. "That was some fine teamwork."

"Not sure if I agree with you," Noel said, stretching out his back and catching his breath.

Bruce gave him a puzzled look. "You don't agree it was teamwork?"

"No, I don't think it weighed less than a bull."

Brody nodded as he leaned up against the other side of the sleigh.

Bruce laughed. "Well, it might've been a bit bigger, but not much."

"While we're here, let's test the frame to see if it's solid." He motioned for Brody to grab his side and the two of them worked in unison to rock the sleigh. It moved just slightly, and no shaking or going askew with their efforts.

"Looks good to me," Bruce said watching from the front, then the back.

"Paint's in good shape over here," Brody said.

Noel ran his hands down his side, with no cracks or flakes appearing. "Same here." He leaned in to run his hand over the leather seats. "The leather is dry as dirt, but I don't see any cracking."

Bruce leaned in to study the seats himself. "That ain't gonna be a problem. I've worked old leather saddles into soft-on-your-butt comfort more than once. I'll need to get it good and clean first, then rub some saddle soap or leather moisturizer into it. Might need to head to the hardware store for enough to get these seats up to snuff."

"Will it be okay out here in the cold?" Noel asked.

"Don't think it'll hurt if for one night, considerin' it's almost been in the elements in that old garage for all these years." He smacked his hand down on the frame once more. Nothing moved. "Since it seems sturdy, I'll let you two get back to fixin' the electrical while I work on cleanin' this. Besides I need to add more firewood to that smoker. Don't want the boss lady mad at me because the temperature dropped on that meat. She's already a bit cranky."

"What's got her cranky?" Noel asked as the trio headed back to the barn.

"Paperwork. She'll ride horses and work with clients all day. Give her bills and the checkbook and she turns a might mean."

"I can't imagine her being mean to anyone."

"You should see her at tax season. Ain't pretty, no sir."

As the other pair went into the barn, Noel stared back at the farmhouse where Monty had shown them her office was the other night. He'd thought the line of credit she'd negotiated with the bank would've had her in good spirits over money, not made it worse.

Chapter Seventeen

Her cell phone rang, breaking up the quiet in her office. Thank goodness. Her eyes were hurting from staring at all these numbers. The fact she had to concentrate so hard to keep them from moving around as she worked, always gave her a headache.

She glanced at the phone call screen. It was Noel's sister-in-law. Monty pushed the speaker phone button.

"Hey, Holly. What's up?"

"I know you're busy cooking brisket for the dinner Saturday night, but I was wondering if you wanted to come over and help Callie and I with a project this evening?"

She glanced out at the late afternoon sun. "I've got all day tomorrow to finish the briskets, so I can certainly come help. What's the project?"

"Buckeyes."

"Buckeyes? Aren't those poisonous nuts, or are we talking about the Ohio State University football team?"

"Neither. It's a tradition in Westen and many other parts of the state to make candy versions of the nuts for the Christmas season."

"Why?" she asked wondering if there was some special connection between the Buckeye nut and Christmas in this part of the country.

Holly laughed. "The recipe makes nine dozen, so most of us make some for ourselves and share the rest with others. I was just hoping you'd come help us this year."

"You know I'm not a baker."

"That's the best part. You don't have to be. Did you ever roll clay into balls as a kid?"

"Sure."

"Then you can make Buckeyes. Why don't you come over about seven. I've got a pot of stew on and biscuits ready to pop into the oven. Between you, me, Callie, Nick and Noel, we should be able to get these made in no time."

"If you're sure you need my help?" she hesitated, not sure she should intrude on a family tradition.

"I do. Someone has to keep my husband and his brother from scarfing them down faster than we can get them made. I'm in no shape to battle them alone."

"I'll come to your rescue then."

As she put on her coat to head outside and check the meat in the smoker, Monty laughed at the idea that two grown men would need to be battled away from some sort of candy by a very pregnant woman. From what she'd seen of Nick and Noel around Holly, the minute she'd snap her fingers they'd jump through hoops to make her happy. At that moment, she decided there was nothing more she'd like to do tonight than to make candy with the Fishers.

After checking one of the slabs of meat with the thermometer, she slipped on her oven mitts and pulled it off the grill rack. She cut off a small slice at one end, then grasping the ends of the slice, she gave it a gentle pull. It easily broke apart into two pieces.

"That smells delicious," Noel said right behind her.

She peeked over her shoulder at him. "Want a taste?"

His face just a few inches from hers, their gazes locked. Her innocent question turned into a suddenly seductive suggestion. Instinctively, she licked her lips in anticipation that he'd take her up on that offer. He leaned closer.

"You thinkin' that meats done?" Bruce said coming around the corner of the house.

Noel took a step back. "I was just asking her the same thing."

Bruce gave them a sure-you-were look, but thankfully refrained from any further comment on how close they'd been. "Best way to determine how good it is, is to give her a taste," he said and held out his hand.

Her cheeks flaming hot from almost being caught in a kiss with Noel, she slapped half the brisket slice into her foreman's hand. She broke the other piece into smaller bites and handed one to Noel. He slipped it in his mouth and closed his eyes as he chewed it, his lips lifting in appreciation of the taste.

"Oh, man," he said, popping his eyes the color of winter spruce open to stare at her. "You weren't kidding. You do know how to make brisket. That tastes amazing."

"Thank you." She slipped her piece into her mouth and tasted it, judging it for tenderness as well as flavor. "I think it's time to get them off the grill."

"You gonna put on the next batch?"

"No, this was the biggest one of the three, so I think we can get the other two done tomorrow. We can let the fire go, clean the grill, and get it all set up for an early start tomorrow."

"Seems a dang waste not to go ahead and cook tonight," Bruce muttered.

"Well, maybe, but I have plans for tonight." Pulling out the clean metal tray she'd brought to store the cooked meat in, she handed it to Noel. "Hold this while I transfer the briskets into it. They need to cool before I put them in the fridge."

"Plans for tonight, huh?" he asked, balancing the tray against his body.

"Yes. Apparently, Holly needs help keeping two bandits out of her Buckeye making process tonight."

"You're coming over tonight?" He sounded surprised and a little tentative.

"Yes, if that's okay?" What if he didn't want her intruding on his family time? Maybe this Buckeye making was something he'd shared with his late wife?

He smiled. "I think that would be great."

She relaxed. "I have one question."

"Shoot."

"What is Buckeye candy made of?"

"Magic deliciousness," he said with a twinkle in his eye.

*
**

"Having fun?" Noel asked Monty as they worked on rolling the last of the Buckeye batter into one-inch balls ready for dipping into chocolate.

"When Holly told me this recipe made nine dozen Buckeyes, which by the way is already a ton of candy, I didn't realize she was making more than one batch."

He laughed and leaned close to whisper. "I think her ambition got out of hand this year. It might be the pregnancy hormones."

"I heard that," his sister-in-law said from her bar stool next to the double-boiler where she and Callie were expertly dipping the peanut butter ball centers into the melted chocolate, leaving the tops uncovered to resemble the Buckeye nut. "I wanted to have something extra to put on the school's table at the festival this weekend. I figure we should have enough for each day, so I tripled the recipe."

"Sweetheart, I think we can all see that." Nick waved at all the trays of candy currently dipped and drying on every counter and the kitchen table.

Holly stuck her tongue out at her husband, who just laughed and went back to bagging the dried candies into bags of six, then tying them off with special red and green colored twist-ties Holly had found online.

"I wish I had thought of this earlier. We could have made up a couple batches at a time and frozen them over the last month."

"I think one night of this was all I could take." Noel popped a peanut butter ball into his mouth.

"How many have you eaten?" Holly asked.

"He owes you for one entire bag full," Monty said, with a laugh.

"Snitch," he teased her. "Besides I saw you eat one of the dipped ones."

"I was taste testing," she said with a smug half smile and a shrug of her shoulders.

He gave her an incredulous look. "It's peanut butter, butter, powdered sugar all rolled into balls and dipped in chocolate. What's to test?"

"I was testing to see if I wanted to buy a bag to take home with me."

"Ah, a taste sample then?"

"Exactly."

"And what did you think, Monty?" Callie asked as she set a tray of the dipped candies onto the counter in exchange for the second to last tray of undipped ones. "Aren't they the best?"

"They're like fancier peanut butter cups. And I think six is more than enough. Although I doubt I'll eat more than one more."

"Why, if you like them so much?" The teenager looked at her like she was crazy.

Monty laughed. "Because the minute Bruce has one, he'll be sneaking the others when he thinks I'm not looking."

"There's a simple fix for that," Noel said.

"What? Hide them? That man sniffs out sweets like a pig does truffles."

"What's a truffle?" Callie asked.

"Well, they're a type of fungus," Holly said from her perch by the stove, and they all laughed at Callie's disgusted face. "Not a gross fungus, but one like mushrooms. And I know you like mushrooms. We get them on pizzas all the time."

"Yeah, but you didn't tell me they were funguses."

"Fungi," Noel corrected her, which got him one of her now patented eyerolls.

"Anyways," Holly continued. "Truffles are very rare because they grown in only certain places, mostly in France and way underground. Truffle farmers train female pigs to search for their scent and that's how they dig them up."

"So, Mr. Bruce has a nose like a pig?" Callie asked.

The adults all laughed.

"No, and don't you say I said that," Monty said. "I meant he can sniff out sweets whenever I have them in the farmhouse. All those cookies you brought last Sunday?"

Callie nodded.

"All gone. Especially those chocolate mint ones."

"Those are my favorites," Callie said, looking a little misty-eyed and Noel knew she was thinking of making those with her mother.

"They're mine too, sweetie," he said as he went over and gave her a little hug.

"So, how far did you get on the barn rewiring?" Nick asked and Noel appreciated the change of subject.

"Pretty good. We disconnected all the outlets and switch boxes, pulled the old wire, ran the wire through about one third of the barn and got the new socket and switches on that part of the barn fixed."

"Why not run all the wire today and work on the reconnects tomorrow?"

"Could've, but Monty wanted to get Percy back in his stall today, so we went this route first."

"What about the other horses? Sugarplum?" Callie asked. "Will they be okay out all night?"

Monty smiled gently at her. "They'll be fine. Remember those places where we put out the hay to feed them?"

"The ones with the little shade roofs built on top?"

"Yes. The horses will gather around those for the night for protection. And Rufus will patrol the area to prevent any predators from trying to sneak in, just like he does when they're all in the barn for the night."

"What kind of predators?" Callie asked.

"Well, in Texas we had to worry about coyotes and some wolves. Here, I think it might just be wolves, although I've never seen one."

"You haven't met Wōden then," Noel said.

Monty turned to him. "Who is Wōden?"

"Wōden is the pet wolf that lives with Deputy Strong and his wife Chloe out in the woods northeast of town."

"He saved Chloe's life," Callie announced.

Holly went on to fill Monty in on the stalker that almost killed Chloe and had shot both Wes and Wōden. "He's been by her side ever since. Even comes to her law office most days."

"So, he's tame?" Monty asked.

"Tame might be stretching it," Nick said. "More like he's adopted Wes and his family, including their son. He's protective of them. I wouldn't want to test him on it."

"Should I be worried about my horses?"

Noel and Nick exchanged looks then both shook their heads. "There haven't been any cows killed by wolves since we've been here. And I'm pretty sure Wes keeps Wōden well fed."

"So, how's that guy you hired working out?" Nick said as they packaged up the last of the Buckeyes.

"Pretty good. Follows directions to the tee. Quick learner. Doesn't talk much."

"I wonder..." Monty said, pausing, contemplating her next words because she wasn't a doctor, just a therapist.

"Wondering what?" Noel prodded her.

"At the ranch in Texas a number of our clients were veterans suffering from Post Traumatic Stress Disorder. Some just appeared lost, unsure where to go with their lives. Unable to move past the things they'd seen or done in war. Some turned to drugs or alcohol to ease their pain and memories. Some were so withdrawn they couldn't make any connections with humans, but working with the animals helped calm them, give them something to trust in again."

"And you believe Brody might have PTSD?" Holly asked.

"I'm not a doctor, so I can't diagnose him as such—"

"But in your professional experience, you're thinking he might be suffering from it?" Nick asked.

Monty gave a shrug. "He might be."

"Is he dangerous?" Noel asked.

"Probably only to himself. Suicide attempts are high in PTSD patients. It's why equine therapy is good for them. They connect with something emotionally and physically. An animal that needs their care as much as they need the animal's."

"Is there anything I can do?" Noel asked.

There it was again, that see a problem fix it mentality he had. Unfortunately, if Brody had PTSD, there wasn't a simple solution to it like putting in a new fuse box. She considered his question. "Since we're just going on pure speculation, I'd say you've already started helping him."

"With a job."

"Yes." She nodded. "And reaching out a hand in friendship. Maybe that will help him start to talk about what's going on and why he's in Westen. Maybe being around the horses will help too."

Noel gave a pessimistic chuckle. "The only horse he's been interested in today was Percy, who has his own animal form of PTSD."

Monty sat up straighter and stared at him. "You are brilliant."

"I am?"

"He is?" Callie, Holly and Nick all said at the same time.

Monty grinned. "Yes. Brody did seem interested in Percy, and Percy even came to the paddock fence where he was standing when he was taking a break."

"Yeah, Brody seemed to like being outside whenever we had to stop. Thought he was just looking for some fresh air."

"Are you saying my barn smells?" she teased.

"It does have a rather ode de manure scent," he teased back.

They stood smiling at each other for a moment.

"Why is Unca Noel and the lady looking so funny?" Gabe asked.

Everyone laughed as Monty and Noel broke their gazes away, her cheeks suddenly flushed. God help her, this man was starting to wiggle his way into her heart.

Chapter Eighteen

"Let's get one of those candy apples," Karl said, pointing to one of the booths up ahead.

"Maybe on the way out," Kurt said, as they slowly walked the aisles of the craft fair.

The building was like a big old barn, except it had lots of booths with people selling things they'd made at home. Lots of Christmas decorations—ornaments, wreaths, and even a three-foot wooden gnome that Karl thought they should get. He'd quickly explained they were just looking, not buying. There were quilts and homemade food stuff. And they stopped at a lot of the booths so they'd look like they fit in with the rest of the crowd milling about. They even spent a long time smelling all the homemade candles at one booth, the lady explaining how she made her candles. That kept Karl busy for a while and let him slowly scan the crowded building.

From what he could see, the place was very busy and lots of people were buying things. If he had to guess, he'd say half were paying in cash, while the others were mostly using credit cards. If they didn't already have a plan, he might consider robbing a few of these people when the fair closed tonight. But that would only be small potatoes and not worth the risk. His original plan was a better payout and he was sticking to it.

"There's a place to get some real food over there," he pointed to the far corner where a bunch of picnic tables were set out. "I think they might have hotdogs and chips."

"And we can sit and go over the plan, right?" his brother grinned at him.

Kurt resisted the urge to punch his brother. The idea was to blend in and not stick out by fighting, but geesh, the kid might as well announce their plans to everyone in town. "We'll talk about it, but quietly and with no one else around to hear. Otherwise, we talk about Christmas, okay?"

"Yeah, yeah. Quiet talk," Karl said, then just like a dog seeing a squirrel, he was distracted again. "Look, it's that guy dressed like Santa and the little elf lady!" He turned right and headed down another aisle to where the big sheriff deputy dressed like Santa and the lady dressed like an elf were having their pictures made with little kids, by one of the other deputies.

"Hey Santa!" Karl called out and Kurt growled softly behind him.

Great! They were trying to be inconspicuous and stay off the police's radar. What does his idiot brother do? Draw the attention of not one, but two lawmen. Might as well hang a sign around their necks announcing, *"We're here to rob your bank"*.

"Hey there! You want to get a picture?" Santa asked.

"No," Kurt said.

"Yes!" Karl said, already walking up to the pair. "C'mon, Kurt. Let's get one together."

Dammit. Now he was in a predicament. Have his picture made and be memorable because two grown guys were hanging out with Santa or make a big deal and raise the suspicions of the deputies?

"C'mon, Kurt!"

Swallowing his ire and his pride, he stalked over to stand with his brother between Santa and the elf. Might as well do the thing that was going to draw the least attention. He'd kill his brother later.

Thankfully, as soon as the picture was done Santa and elf were swarmed by a group of school kids, so Kurt dragged Karl away before he could get into a question and answer session with the pair.

"Let's go get something to eat," he said almost pulling his brother away.

They settled on three hotdogs, two bags of chips and a drink each. Kurt picked out a table not in the back corner, but away from the other occupied tables, not only to keep others from hearing them discuss the steps of their plans, but to keep Karl from getting distracted. If he could keep his brother focused as they talked, he wouldn't have to repeat anything. If not, he'd never get past step two.

He waited until they'd both finished their first hot dogs. "We need to make our move on Sunday."

Karl swallowed the food in his mouth. "But banks are closed on Sundays."

"You're right. They are, but remember, we're not going inside to rob the bank this time. We're getting the manager to give us the money."

"For his daughter." Karl nodded and took another bite of food.

"Shhh. Not so loud." Kurt looked around to be sure no one had heard what his brother said. Several couples and families were at the picnic tables. The closest one to them were three ladies, two tall ones and one shorter one. They were drinking and talking while their babies were asleep in their strollers and a little boy played with a plastic ball. No one gave him or his brother much notice. *Good.* "We need to get the girl Sunday night and give her dad the message to bring us the money on Monday when the bank's open."

"And we're going to have to spend the night out in that old creepy house in the woods."

Fear entered his brother's eyes. The same kind he used to see when their mother would lock them out of the house at night when she was entertaining her clients. He hated to see Karl scared.

"Yes, but we checked it out during the day, the other day, remember, when we drove by that horse farm. There are windows, a cot we put the sleeping bag on and those old chairs. We just have to be there one night. And we'll be together." He stared at his brother as he spoke in a calm, reassuring voice, just like he did when they were kids. Slowly the fear and panic left his face. "It will be worth it when we get the money and can go to Florida."

"Where it's warm all year," Karl said with a grin, his fear replaced with joy. For years they'd planned out all the theme parks they'd attend and going to the beach.

Suddenly there was a high-pitched squeal and the little boy jumped off his seat to chase the plastic ball as it bounced toward the brothers. Karl jumped off his seat to catch it first, making the little boy stop a few feet away and stare up at him.

"This your ball?" Karl asked, squatting down

The boy nodded, his dark hair bobbing a bit. The shorter of the three ladies started towards him, watching Karl and Kurt like any wary mother should.

"Want it back?"

"Please," the child said.

Karl smiled and bounced it his way. "Catch it."

He did and squealed with delight, showing the ball to his mother, who took his hand. "Thank you," she said to Karl and headed back to their table.

Kurt ground his teeth. The last thing he wanted to do was draw attention to themselves. Now this lady will remember Karl bouncing the ball back to her kid. The sooner they snatched the girl, got the money and got the hell out of the town the better. It was a solid plan and if they stuck to it, nothing could go wrong. "Finish eating. We'll drive out there again, just to be sure no one else has found the place. I don't want you scared of it, okay?"

*
**

"That's the last one," Noel said, tightening the final screw on the electrical socket next to the tack room. He and Brody had come full circle with the rewiring of Monty's barn and training facility. He stepped away and nodded at his helper. "You can flip the circuit breaker back on now."

"You sure?" Brody asked, hesitating.

Noel nodded. "If we did everything right, the system should be good to go."

"Okay, you're the boss." Brody switched the circuit breaker to on and wha-la, light flooded the barn.

Clapping came from behind them.

"Good job!" Monty stood with Beth and her mother in the barn's opening, snow falling behind them like they were standing in a huge snow globe someone had shaken.

"Thank you, ladies. Couldn't have gotten it done this quickly without Brody," Noel said, turning to high-five his helper. For a moment he thought the other man would leave him hanging and feeling like a fool, but he only hesitated before slapping hands with him in celebration of their accomplishment.

Progress.

In the two and a half days since they'd been working together, Noel hadn't been able to pry more than work related

137

conversation from Brody. On their lunch breaks he made it clear he wasn't going to talk about his past. Other than their shared surprise over finding the sleigh in the old garage, the only animation he'd seen in the other man was when he watched Percy in the outdoor paddock or in his stall. The weird thing about that was the horse seemed just as curious about Brody.

"Can we bring Sugarplum inside now?" Beth asked Monty, worry apparent on her face.

"Of course we can. I'm sure all the horses will be glad to get in out of this snow." Monty looked around, then focused on Noel. "Have you seen Bruce?"

Noel shrugged as non-committal as he could, not wanting to give away the old cowboy's surprise, and shook his head. "Not since lunch."

As if on cue, the sound of sleigh bells grew closer, then Sugarplum appeared outside the front entrance to the barn, pulling the freshly cleaned horse sleigh with Bruce holding the reins.

"Sugarplum!" Beth happily jumped up and down then rushed over to the horse.

"Careful Beth!" her mother called and hurried after her.

Beth stopped two feet away from the horse. Smiling, she lifted her arm and waited. Sugarplum leaned her nose down to nuzzle Beth's hand. Her giggle rang out.

"She trusts her," Brody said, sounding surprised.

"Which one?" Noel asked.

Brody didn't stop watching the pair. "Both."

"That's what Beth's therapy has done for her," Monty said, then headed to where Bruce climbed off the sleigh. "Where did you get this?"

Noel followed her.

"Found it in your garage. Those two," Bruce said nodding

Noel and Brody's direction, "helped me get her out. Cleaned her up while tending your brisket fire."

Sugarplum shook her head and bells jangled.

"Oh, she has sleigh bells," Beth said excitedly, which got her another shake of the horse's head. Apparently, Sugarplum liked them as much as Beth did.

"I found those in the garage too," Bruce said, looking quite pleased with himself. "A bit of spit and polish and dressed our lady here up real nice."

Beth made a face. "Eww, you spit on them?"

Bruce chuckled. "No. I used soap and water and elbow grease. Got them all shiny lookin' just so Sugarplum could wear them to the tree lightin' party tonight. But I have a problem."

Beth leaned in closer. "What problem?"

"I need someone to go on a test drive with her and I to see how the sleigh works. Don't suppose you know anyone who'd want to be doin' that, do you?"

"I do! I do!" Beth said, then turned to her mother. "Mom, can I test the sleigh with Mr. Bruce?"

"Your mom can come too."

Bruce and Beth looked hopefully at her mother, who laughed.

"I haven't been on an old fashioned sleigh ride in years. Why not," she said and climbed up with Beth into the back seat. Bruce produced an old red and black plaid quilt to drape over their legs. "Don't want ya gettin' too chilled out in this snow."

Once they were settled, Bruce climbed into the front seat and gave the reins a little shake, filling the air with the jangling bells, then the mare started across the snowy field at a light trot, the sleigh gliding smoothly along behind her. Noel and Monty walked out onto the drive to watch them as the snow kept falling.

Brody headed for his car, having driven himself to the worksite today. Noel had paid him in cash an hour earlier for the hours he'd worked, telling him if he was interested in more to come to the office on Monday and they'd get him assigned to one of their other jobs in progress. Brody hadn't committed, nor had he refused.

"Brody," Monty called, stopping him.

"Yes, ma'am?" he asked.

"If you'd like to come out to see Percy again, you're welcome anytime. I know he'd like it."

For a moment he stood rock still and Noel thought he'd refuse.

"I'll think about it," he finally said before climbing in his car and driving off.

He pulled out and left without any kind of wave.

Just after he turned off the drive onto the road, an old sedan drove near the fence in the same direction as the sleigh, but Sugarplum, with Bruce guiding her by the reins, didn't appear the least bit phased as it passed by on her left.

"How did I not see Bruce working on the sleigh?" Monty asked.

"He wanted it to be a surprise," Noel said. "In case it was a bust, he didn't want to get your hopes up."

She turned and gave him a curious look. "My hopes up about the sleigh? I didn't even know it existed until just now."

"Bruce has the idea that you could add some income by giving sleigh rides to customers during the winter months. Especially since the weather will probably keep you from giving riding lessons this winter."

"I know southwest Pennsylvania gets around four feet of snow most winters, but not every year. Is it the same here in Ohio?" she asked, walking back into the barn and opened up the closest stall.

Noel followed her. "Seems we get about three or four feet

140

over the entire winter, but the farmer's Almanac is predicting heavier accumulation this year and earlier." He waved at the door behind them. "As evidenced by the snows we've been having all week."

A horse whinnied. Monty's assistant trainer Camden led two of the horses they boarded into the barn. Noel moved out of the way so he could put one into the open stall, while Monty housed the second one

Cam removed the lead rope and closed the stall door. "Two down, four more to go," the younger man said and jogged back out of the barn.

"You're bringing in all the horses then?" Noel asked as Monty went to open the other stall doors. "I thought you said the cold won't bother them unless it's below twenty?"

She smiled at him. "You were paying attention."

Since the day they'd met, there wasn't anything this woman said or did that he wasn't paying attention to. What could he say? She fascinated him. He watched as she and her trainer housed all the horses, making sure they were secure for the night.

When they were finished, they all went to the barn exit and she turned off the lights for the night. "Just like you and I can tolerate the cold weather with our winter coats, it also feels nice to be out of the cold, wind and snow in a nice warm place, doesn't it? Same with the horses. Besides, since we're all going to the play and tree lighting ceremony this evening, having the horse secured inside the barn will make Rufus' job of guarding them a little easier." She called the dog and said, "Protect."

Rufus loped into the barn and climbed onto the blanket covered pile of hay that was his guard spot near the entrance.

"So, you're coming to the Jubilee kickoff tonight?" Noel asked after Camden climbed in his truck and drove off.

"I haven't really had a chance to get into town and visit the shops, although I do love how everything looked the other day when we had lunch and I picked up the brisket meat. And I definitely want to hear Callie sing in the play."

Noel couldn't hide the pride in his daughter. "She's not one of the characters this year. That's only for elementary school kids. But it's become a tradition for her to sing O Holy Night at the end. It brings tears to my eyes at how beautifully she sings it. She sounds just like her mother when she does."

Monty laid her hand on his arm. "Then I definitely want to hear her tonight."

Still fighting his emotions, he stared down into her blue eyes. "She'd love that. And now you have your own special sleigh to come to town in," he said as Bruce slowed the sleigh to a stop in front of them.

"Is Sugarplum coming to the Jubilee tonight?" Beth asked as she and her mother climbed out of the sleigh.

Monty laughed. "I guess so, but we'll need to let her rest a while. She's never pulled a sleigh before today."

"Can I ride in the sleigh again?"

"Beth," her mother made eye-contact with her daughter. "Miss Monty knows how to care for Sugarplum. If she brings her and the sleigh to the Jubilee tonight, you'll get to see them there. And I suspect, she'll be letting people sign up for rides out here at the farm and not in town. Am I right?" she asked glancing at Monty.

She exchanged looks with Bruce. "I believe that is the plan. But I guarantee, you'll get to take another sleigh ride."

Beth made a little pouty face, then reached over to shake the cloth with the sleigh bells sewn on and make them jingle. "I guess I can wait." Then she looked at Noel. "Will Callie be at the Jubilee tonight?"

He nodded. "She will be. She's singing a solo at the end of the play."

"I heard her sing last year," Beth said. "It was pretty. She's a good singer."

"She practices a lot," he said, glancing at his watch. "In fact, she's practicing her song at the play's dress rehearsal right now."

"What's a dress rehearsal?" Beth asked.

"That's when all the people in the play put on their costumes and do the play without any audience watching," her mother said.

Beth giggled. "That's silly. You're supposed to have people there to watch the show."

Noel chuckled. "I agree, it sounds silly. But they do it this way to be sure there are no mistakes in their play and the show tonight can go off without any problems."

Beth grew very serious. "No one likes problems."

Noel had to agree with her. Hopefully, all the festivities tonight would go out without any kind of catastrophe.

Chapter Nineteen

"You sounded so good," Monty told Callie when she joined them after the play finished. She and Bruce arrived by sleigh in plenty of time to take the seats Noel saved them in the front row, next to his brother and nephew.

"You did a great job, kiddo," Noel said, hugging his daughter.

As was the Friday night tradition, the civic center was packed for the first performance with family and friends of the kids in the play, all of whom had changed out of their costumes already. Although the boy who'd played Scrooge, still had remnants of green paint on his face from his superhero character. The town's many leaders, including Mayor Maggie and Sheriff Justice and their families were here for the opening of the play.

"I really liked the high note," Beth said, coming up beside them with her parents and giving Callie a hug too. The girls had quickly bonded over their love of horses, especially Sugarplum.

"I was a little nervous," Callie said, a shyness at all the

compliments making her blush. "But just like every year, I remembered Mom singing the song at church, so I just pretended she was on the stage with me, and all my nervousness went away."

"What a good way to overcome the butterflies," Monty said, and Callie beamed at her.

"It's too cold for butterflies," Beth said looking curiously at them both.

"Yes, it is," Callie said and gave her new friend a hug as she patiently explained. "It's something people say when you're really nervous. It's like you have butterflies fluttering around in your stomach."

"Like the first time I sat on Sugarplum's back? It was so high up and my stomach felt all funny."

Callie nodded. "That's what they call butterflies in your stomach."

"Do you get butterflies when you sing? I don't think I would if I could sing that really high note like you do."

"Sometimes I do at the beginning. That's when I think of my mom and the butterflies go away. By the time I get to that note near the end, I'm just so happy it makes the note seem easy to sing."

"It's my favorite part," Beth said.

Callie grinned. "Mine too." She looked up when some friends called to her. She waved and reached for her coat Noel held. "Dad, can I go with Rowan and the others to the tree lighting ceremony?"

He appeared to consider her request. Monty noticed that he often hesitated before replying to his daughter. She suspected it was as much to let the girl know he considered her requests important enough to take them seriously, as well as whether something was safe or not.

"You'll stay in the group and not wander off?" he asked.

"Yes," she said, pulling her coat on.

"And stay within sight of me or your aunt and uncle?"

This time he was met with the teenager eye roll and nod. "Yes."

"Okay. You can go."

She grinned, then turned to Beth. "Want to come meet my best friend Rowan?"

Beth nodded, then looked at her parents. "Can I?"

Her parents exchanged a hopeful, but worried look. Their normally, very shy daughter was asking to venture off without them, even if it was going to be a few feet away. Something she never would've done without her therapy sessions and making a new friend in Callie. Finally, Beth's father inhaled slightly and gave a nod.

"Of course, you can," her mother said. "But you stay with Callie, okay?"

Beth bobbed her head and grinned at Callie who took her hand and headed over to Rowan, the Lewis twins and several other teens. Monty moved to stand by Beth's mom. "She's making progress."

"I know," Vanessa said, with a bit of a catch in her voice. "It's what we wanted. For her to make friends and not need us quite so much."

"Well," her husband said, taking her hand. "Let's go join the party outside."

"Sounds like a plan," Noel said, moving beside Monty. "Bruce said he was going to check on Sugarplum, then join us."

"Don't you have to light the lights on the tree?" she asked as they walked behind Beth's family and the group of young teens to the town square two blocks from the civic center.

"Nope. I've got it all rigged to light from the top down when

Mayor Maggie pushes the button. I get to enjoy them light up with everyone else."

As they neared the town square, people seemed to be streaming in from all directions, not just those who had attended the first night of the Jubilee play. Many were from the holiday marketplace, as well as the local stores, that were closing for the night, so their employees could join the tree lighting ceremony. Monty understood Noel's concern that his daughter at least consider her safety a little with this crowd forming. With both town folks and visitors in the square, she felt a little crowded in herself.

The group of teens stopped about five feet from the huge, decorated evergreen tree in the center of the square. It was stationed just a few yards from the gazebo which, was also decorated for the holidays. On the other side of the gazebo stood the six-foot tall Hanukkah menorah that would have its first candle lit next week on the first day of that holiday. Noel maneuvered them to stand a few feet away from the teens. Beth's parents and her younger brothers joined them.

"It looks lovely," Monty said.

"I haven't seen it all decorated," Noel said beside her.

She stared up at him in surprise. "You haven't? I thought you did all the lights on it."

He leaned in so she could hear him over the crowd. "My team did. We placed the lights the same day we did the lights along main street. The rest of the decorating committee placed all the ornaments and bows. They did a great job. Hope the lighting lives up to it."

"I'm sure it will."

Just then the crowd started cheering as Mayor Maggie Landon stepped onto the stage constructed at the base of the tree. Nick helped Holly up onto the stage, then stood below it with their son in his arms.

"Hello everyone!" she called out and received resounding hellos back. "Welcome to the ninety-third Yuletide Jubilee celebration!"

Cheers and applause filled the air.

"Did you get to see the children's play tonight? Wasn't it great?"

"Yes!" many of the crowd, including Monty and Noel shouted back.

"Scrooge was a hulking big star this year!" the actor's father called out, his son still having green pain all over his face.

"He was a smashing success!" Maggie said to the delight of all the audience. "As tradition would have it, we're going to have two ceremonies tonight. First, we're going to light the Christmas tree. We'll sing some carols, then we're going to lift the Yuletide Kissing Bough in the gazebo."

More cheering resounded, with many people calling out who they wanted to kiss under that huge mistletoe ball this year.

"So, let's light our tree. Count down with me from five," the Mayor said holding the button to light the tree lights in her hand, high over her head for everyone to see. "Five! Four! Three! Two! One! Merry Christmas!"

She pushed the button.

There was a slight pause as nothing happened. A chuckle from beside her, told Monty that Noel had planned the delay.

Suddenly the star at the top shone as bright as the original star in Bethlehem must've shone on that first Christmas all those years ago. Then bright colors of twinkling lights cascaded like a waterfall down the tree on all sides. The audience bursting out in applause and amazement.

"Oooo!"

"Ahhh!"

"Wow!"

"You did that on purpose," Monty said, so just Noel could hear her.

He leaned down and grinned at her, his face mere inches from hers. "It was worth the suspense, wasn't it?"

She laughed. "You had everyone wondering if it was going to happen."

"Great job, Dad!" Callie yelled a few feet in front of them.

"Now Mrs. Holly Fisher will lead us in some Christmas Carols. You were all given handouts with the words, in case any of them are unfamiliar to you. Holly?"

Holly took the microphone. "Since we just lit the tree, how about we start with O *Christmas Tree*?" She hummed a long note, then began singing. Everyone joined in, and for four or five songs, everyone sang.

Monty moved her lips to the words, listening to all the people around her.

"You're not singing," Noel whispered halfway through the third carol."

"Tone deaf, remember?"

"You weren't joking?" he asked, surprise written on his face.

She slowly shook her head. "Nope. Not kidding."

Without thinking, he wrapped his arm around her and hauled her up beside him. "I'll sing for both of us."

Monty blinked hard at the sudden tears that filled her eyes. Her family had teased her about her inability to carry a tune to even a simple song like O *Christmas Tree*. Kids at school made fun of her to the point that she never sang again. Yet, here was this man she'd only known a few weeks, and he was holding her close enough to feel the words rumble in his chest, almost as if she were singing along.

At the end of the caroling, Mayor Maggie took the microphone once more. "If you'll turn to your left and face the gazebo, Deputy Strong and Deputy Löwe will raise the Yuletide Kissing

Bough. Remember, you have until midnight Christmas Eve to kiss your true love beneath it, no need to rush the gazebo tonight."

Laughter and whistles sounded from the crowd, with a couple of football players elbowing each other near the cheerleaders.

"On the count of three deputies," the mayor said. "One. Two. Three!"

The deputies pulled on the ropes at the same time the mayor pushed another button setting the ball of mistletoe and ribbons glowing in white Christmas lights. Oohs, aahs and applause rang out.

Mayor Maggie got everyone's attention again. "Don't forget to shop at the Yuletide Jubilee marketplace tomorrow and Sunday. Get your tickets for the last two performances of the children's play tomorrow and Sunday afternoons. We'll be lighting the menorah every night of Hanukkah starting next week. And tomorrow night there will be the holiday dinner and dance. Rumor has it we're having some real Texas barbecued brisket. If you haven't gotten your tickets yet, be sure to get them so you won't miss out. I hope to see you there."

The crowd applauded again, then started to breakup, although many small groups still wandered around the square.

"Excellent job on the lighting," Sheriff Justice said, as he and his family approached Monty, Noel and Beth's parents, still standing close enough to watch the group of laughing teens.

Callie made sure Beth was included in the group, which made Monty as proud of her as if she were her own daughter. The girl's enthusiasm about riding and training horses had warmed her heart, but it was Callie's acceptance of Beth, despite her Down's Syndrome, that proved the girl's inner strength. The fact the other teens hadn't bulked at Beth joining them at Callie's insistence spoke of her leadership.

Noel may not yet know it, but he'd raised a remarkable young woman.

"There was a moment, when I thought it wouldn't work," Bobby Justice said beside her husband and they all laughed. "Was it intentional?"

Noel shrugged. "Mostly to make my brother nervous. He's been bugging me about it needing to go off without a hitch."

"I knew it!" Nick said as he, Holly and little Gabriel joined them.

The four little boys began to play tag in the snow around their parents, just as Callie came running back with her friends following.

"Beth says you rode a sleigh to town, Monty," she said. "Can we go see it, Dad?"

Noel hesitated.

"It's just on the other side of the marketplace." Monty said, then leaned closer. "Bruce was going to check on it and Sugarplum."

That seemed to sway his decision. "Okay, but stay together."

The kids excitedly headed to the marketplace building. Noel kept his gaze on his daughter until all the kids disappeared around the corner.

*
**

"Hey Jay," Gage said to Beth's father. "I'm going to have Jason standing guard outside the nightly drop box over at the bank tonight and tomorrow, if that's okay with you."

The bank manager tensed with alert interest, which drew all the adults' attention. "Something up, Sheriff?"

"Remember that flier I brought by a few days ago?"

"The one about the rash of bank robberies? Has there been more?"

151

Gage shook his head. "No, and that's what has me worried. The pair have moved from the far northeast Ohio steadily south, making a circle around us Last bank job was two weeks ago, then nothing."

"You think they mean to hit our bank?"

Gage slowly perused the town square with all the holiday decorations, then shifted to the large marketplace, also decorated with lights and wreaths. Finally, he focused on Jay once more. "This is the one time of the year when we're completely flooded with tourists and out-of-towners. It's also one of the biggest weekends for the town to profit off the small town holiday craft fair. As you're well aware, the town makes tons of money this weekend."

"All of which gets deposited each night into the bank's local night drop slot," Jay said, understanding the sheriff's concern. "Do you suspect them already being here? We are due the quarterly payment from the state in our system tomorrow."

In the last month of every yearly quarter the state sent a deposit to the bank of physical funds to be used by the town and county for continued upgrades as part of their reparations for the FUBAR that occurred because of one of their DEA administrators and the rogue state justice DA—who happened to be Gage's ex-wife—that led to the near annihilation of Westen when the underground meth lab exploded on the outskirts of the town. Due to the fourth quarter ending in December, the state always sent the payment early. The fact the deposit was occurring the day after the Yuletide Jubilee weekend was another reason Gage's spidey-sense acted like a five-alarm fire was going to happen.

He laid one hand on the other man's shoulder. "Let's just say I'm erring on the side of caution. We'll have someone there armed and dressed in uniform to protect all the shop proprietors and crafters as they deposit their money each night. And I'll double the team inside the bank on Monday too."

Jay nodded, relaxing a little. "Give a show of force before someone decides to try and rob someone. Sort of warn them away."

"Right. I believe we should try to scare someone off from doing something stupid they'll regret later."

Chapter Twenty

"Look, Callie," Beth said, tugging on her hand as they rounded the marketplace building. "Isn't it beautiful?"

Callie agreed. It was like something out of an old book or movie. A red sleigh with Christmas decorations strung on it and at the front stood Sugarplum ready to pull it through the snow. She reached up to stroke the horse's mane which jiggled the sleighbells draped over her neck.

"It's way cool," Brian Lewis said.

"And you got to ride in it?" his twin brother Ben asked.

"This afternoon with my mom," Beth said, running her hand over the sleigh. "Mr. Bruce took us around the farm."

"I wish I could ride in it," Rowan said.

Beth smiled. "Mr. Bruce said Monty was going to give sleigh rides at the farm."

"Oh, man! Let's go ask her if we can go on one!" Ben said, his brother high-fiving him.

"Yeah! Let's go on one tomorrow!"

Rowan was just as excited. "How about tonight?"

The trio started off back to the square.

"Sugarplum can't be alone," Beth said reaching over to rub the horse's nose.

"You coming, Callie?" Rowan called.

She wanted to go with her friends, but Beth was her friend too, and she couldn't leave her alone. "I think I'll stay with Sugarplum until Mr. Bruce comes back too."

Beth smiled at her.

"Okay, we'll find out about the rides and sign you up. Okay?" Rowan yelled.

"Thank you!" Callie called back then stroked her hand down the horse's back making her shake her head a little and jingle the bells once more. She and Beth laughed.

"She likes the jingles," Beth said.

"Like she's calling Santa," Callie said. "Hey, Santa, I'm ready to go and I can run faster than your reindeer!"

"I can give you a ride," a voice said from behind them, startling both girls.

Callie turned, instinctively coming between the man—well, he might be just an older teen. He sort of looked like some of the high schoolers she knew—and Beth. "Uhm, no, we're just waiting for Mr. Bruce to come be with Sugarplum."

"Oh, he's busy right now. Asked me to keep an eye on the horse and sleigh. I'm Karl." He moved closer with a sort of crooked grin. "Mr. Bruce showed me how to drive the horse."

Beth scooted around Callie, grinning up at the stranger. "You mean the sleigh?"

"Yeah," he said, going around them and climbing into the front seat. "You want to go another ride?"

"Yes!" Beth said, already scrambling into the backseat. "C'mon, Callie!"

She hesitated. Karl was a stranger and she'd promised her dad she'd be right here.

155

"You don't have to come," Karl said, picking up the reins. "I'll bring her right back."

Callie knew she should tell Beth to get down, but her friend looked so happy. She couldn't let her go alone though. So, she climbed up into the seat, just as Karl snapped the reins, and suddenly she was thrown back against the leather as Sugarplum took off in a gallop, almost tipping the sleigh over.

"Slow down!" she yelled, grabbing a hold of the side of the sleigh with one hand and Beth with the other, cursing herself for a stupid decision. If this guy didn't drive them into a tree, her dad was going to kill her.

*
**

"Let's go collect our girls," Noel said to Jay after Gage and Bobby headed to join her sisters' families near the hot chocolate stand.

"I have to say, when Vanessa brought up the idea of Beth taking riding lessons as part of her therapy, I was a little leery," Jay said as they wove their way through the crowded square. "But the change in her was almost overnight."

Vanessa nodded in agreement. "A year ago, she would've been too shy to even talk to other kids. Now she's part of the group."

"Working with the horses and meeting your daughter has been good for Callie too," Noel said, then smiled at Monty. "Her attitude has been a lot more pleasant that's for sure."

"Monty!" the Lewis twins yelled running in their direction. "Can we sign up for sleigh rides?"

Rowan was running with them. "Me too! Can we make it a big group?"

The four adults stopped as Monty was surrounded by the trio.

"I haven't planned for those this weekend," Monty was saying, but Noel's attention was the corner of the marketplace, expecting to see Callie come running after her friends. But she didn't.

"Where's Beth?" Vanessa asked, worry in her voice.

"She wanted to stay with Sugarplum at the sleigh until Mr. Bruce came back," Rowan said.

"And Callie?" Noel asked.

Rowan gave a shrug. "She didn't want Beth to stay by herself. I promised to sign her up for the rides."

No longer hearing the teen, concern, bordering on panic, surged through Noel. He broke away from the group and strode in the direction his daughter had gone. He heard footsteps behind him and glanced to see Jay keeping pace, the same concern on his face.

She was safe. He was going overboard. He'd told her to stay there and she'd do what he told her too. He'd also told her to stay with the group.

They turned the corner.

The only thing moving was Bruce stumbling in from the dark, holding his head. Blood coursing down his face.

The sleigh was gone.

The girls were gone.

Chapter Twenty-One

"**B**ruce!" Monty gasped as she came around the corner of the marketplace to see her friend leaning against the side of the building. The local streetlight shining through the new falling snow to show the blood oozing down the left side of his face. Noel was helping him sink to the ground.

"Go get Gage and some help," Noel said to Jay, who ran past Monty as she hurried over to squat down in front of her foreman.

"What happened?" she asked, opening her bag and pulling a tissue out of the small package she kept inside. She carefully dabbed at the blood, working at the lowest point and up towards the gash on his left temple.

Bruce squinted up at her. "Young feller was askin' me about the sleigh and how it worked. Seemed like an okay sort, a little slow. So, I let him climb up onto the seat, showed him the reins. Next thing I knew, I was layin' over in the alley behind this buildin', my head achin' like someone hit it with a sledgehammer."

"Did you see Callie and Beth?" Noel asked bending over to look the older man in the face.

"Not since she was up on that stage singin' like an angel. Why?"

Noel didn't wait to explain but jogged down the side road in the direction the sleigh had gone.

"They came to see the sleigh and Sugarplum," Monty said, watching Noel with an ache and worry in her heart. She wanted to run after the girls with him, but she could only solve one problem at a time. Right this minute Bruce needed looking after. Turning her attention back to him, she carefully dabbed away more of the blood closer to the gash on his left temple.

"Here let me take a look," a pretty blonde lady said, squatting down beside Monty and shining a flashlight at Bruce's cut. She recognized her as Bobby Justice's sister Dylan, a doctor over at the hospital. "You're going to need some stitches there, sir."

Behind them a crowd gathered. Noel had run back up the street to join them and was telling the sheriff what had happened and that the girls were missing.

Bruce leaned to the side. "Where's Sugarplum and the sleigh? That scallywag must've taken them." He tried to stand, but the doctor laid her hand on his shoulder to hold him down.

"You need to sit still and let me check you out. You might have a concussion."

"I need to find our horse and those girls," he said, but didn't try to move again.

"We'll find them," Monty said. "You need to stay here and let the doctor check you out. Please?"

Bruce's face softened and he nodded. "I'm sorry I let him get on the sleigh, boss."

"It will be okay," she said patting his arm, praying she wasn't lying. Then she went over to hear what the plan was to find the girls.

"Bruce said it was a young man. Maybe a little slow mentally?" Monty said as the men studied the trail the sleigh had left heading up the street northeast away from town.

"The snow's going to cover the tracks. We've got to get going," Jay said, sounding frantic.

Noel grabbed him by the arm. "Don't feed into the panic. It's not going to help either of the girls."

"But Beth...she's not going to know what to do out alone in the cold and the dark," the other man's eyes had bleak despair in them, his wife stood beside him, clutching both her sons' hands.

"Callie's with her," Monty said.

"That's not terribly reassuring," Jay snapped, and Monty knew it was only his fear for his daughter that caused him to do it.

"Callie has a good head on her shoulders, and she'll stick close to Beth, no matter what," Noel said with great confidence in his daughter. Monty knew it was as much for his own reassurance as Jay and Vanessa's. She didn't know if he'd appreciate it, but she slipped her hand in his to will him some strength and to ease her own worry over both girls. Without looking down, he simply squeezed her hand and held on tight.

"But why did this guy take them?" the young deputy Jason asked, standing by the sheriff and his wife.

The crowd was growing by the minute. Everyone voiced their opinions and questions at the same time. None of it bringing the girls back any quicker. Monty felt the tension in Noel growing and she moved just a little closer. She wanted to wrap her arms around this strong man and reassure him everything would be okay, but until his daughter was safely home with him, she knew the words would ring hollow.

A sudden whistle split the air. Everyone turned to see who'd made the noise.

Lorna Doone.

"Pipe down and give the sheriff a chance to talk," she said and waved a hand back towards Gage.

He gave her a nod in thanks. "As you've heard, we've had two girls go missing. We suspect they've been taken in a horse driven sleigh heading northeast out of town. They have about a fifteen minute head start on us. From the new snowfall, you can see the stormfront is moving through and temperatures are going to drop, so time is of the essence."

*
**

What was going on?

Kurt slowly neared the crowd of people gathering near the marketplace building. The spot where he told Karl to wait for him while he moved their car across from the café. The alley there had no streetlight directly on it which made it a great place to sneak their prey away from the festivities. The less commotion when they snatched her, the easier for them to get away unnoticed.

The idea to move their plan forward to tonight hit him as he and Karl hung around for the tree lighting ceremony and watched all the people. There must've been hundreds milling around the square. It made sense to take the banker's daughter tonight when no one would realize she was gone until they were out of town and at the hideout shack.

Now, something else was going on.

A whistle silenced all the talking and the big Sheriff held up his hands.

Kurt moved closer to hear what he was saying.

"...we've had two girls go missing. We suspect they've been taken in a horse driven sleigh heading northeast out of town. They have about a fifteen minute head start on us. From the new snowfall, you can see the stormfront is moving through and temperatures are going to drop, so time is of the essence."

Oh shit. Shit. Shit. What the hell did Karl do?

He wanted to run to the car and get out of town. But he had to see what their plans were. Did they know about the hideout? Did Karl know how to get there? How the hell had he gotten the girl? No wait, they said girls.

In his panic he'd started pacing. Suddenly, he slammed into someone.

"Excuse me," she said, stepping around him. It was the lady whose little boy had tossed the ball at him and Karl yesterday. She paused and looked at him. "Are you okay?"

He froze. "Uh, yeah. Yeah."

She nodded and hurried up into the crowd.

"The person who took the girls is driving a horse drawn sleigh, which means he doesn't have to stay on the roads," the sheriff said.

Crap! Karl took the sleigh? How? He didn't know the first thing about horses or sleighs. He stole a horse! Didn't they hang horse thieves? What the hell was he going to do?

Chapter Twenty-Two

"I'm scared," Beth whispered beside Callie, who was holding her with one hand while she used the other to grip the side of the sleigh and hold them inside as they bumped and flew over the snowy landscape.

"I am too, but our dads will find us," she whispered back. One thing she knew for sure, if her dad knew she'd been kidnapped by a crazy guy with a sleigh, he'd do whatever it took to find her. "We just have to hold on to each other, okay, Beth?"

Beth nodded and clutched her hand tighter.

Dad always told her to be aware of her surroundings and if the little voice in her head told her something was wrong, to listen to it. Why hadn't she listened when that voice told her not to get in the sleigh?

Because Beth was already in it.

Something else Dad told her, *"Always look out for people who are vulnerable or are weaker than you."* Beth was sweet, but way too trusting and very vulnerable to someone like the maniac driving this thing. No one else was there to help protect her. That's why she'd climbed into the sleigh.

Yes, she was scared. Who wouldn't be riding what felt like a rollercoaster that was off the rails? And the snow, that she usually loved to watch fall, was getting harder and the wind blowing it in like one of those snow globes she loved to shake up. Worse though, she was scared of what would happen when they stopped? What did this guy want?

All the headlines she'd seen on the news and internet stories about things that people did to kids roared through her brain, making her heart race almost as fast as Sugarplum was galloping.

Sugarplum. Did this guy know how to slow her down?

She wished she had had more riding lessons, then she might know how to slow the mare's pace. Surely, she'd get tired at some point, wouldn't she?

And as if Sugarplum read her thoughts, the sleigh slowed.

Callie swallowed hard and relaxed her hold on the sleigh just a little bit. Then she breathed in and exhaled slowly a couple of times —something Aunt Holly had told her to do to stop her anxiety when singing in front of people. A way to give herself some courage.

"Where are you taking us?" she asked the guy holding the reins.

"To the hideout," he said, glancing over his shoulder at them. His eyes were wide, like someone scared as much as her. He looked over the other shoulder, then back the other way, as if he was trying to figure out where they were. "It's in the trees. That's where Kurt showed me."

Callie considered where they were. They'd headed out of town past the original town and on the opposite side of Westen where her family lived. The forest were thicker here. The Gentle Creek Ranch was south on this side of the county. But the driver wasn't taking them that way. He was heading North and if he kept going, they'd come to some of the Amish farms near Mayor Maggie's Christmas Tree farm and holiday shop that was out this way. She'd been there just last month with Aunt Holly.

"Which trees?" Callie asked, hoping if he talked to her, he'd calm down.

"They were on the right." He pulled on the right rein and made Sugarplum turn that direction.

Dang it. He was heading away from the farms. She didn't know where they were, the only light was the glow off the snow-covered landscape they were traveling on. Suddenly, a dark wall of trees sprang up in front of them.

"Whoa!" the guy said pulling on the reins to bring Sugarplum to a stop just before they crashed into a large evergreen.

Before she knew it, the guy jumped off the front of the sleigh.

He pulled a gun from his pocket and pointed it at Callie. "I don't need you. You stay here!" He grabbed a hold of Beth, pulling her down off the back seat beside him. "You come with me."

Beth started crying as he dragged her by the arm into the woods. "No. I don't want to. I want to go home. Callie!"

"Wait!" Callie said, scrambling out of the sleigh. "She's scared. I have to come with her!"

He swung around and pointed the gun at Callie, stopping her by Sugarplum. "You can come with us, but don't give me any trouble."

"I won't." She started around Sugarplum, her hand running over her mane to soothe the mare. An idea hit her. "I need to bring the sleigh bells," she said, pulling off the collar of bells the collar.

"Why?"

"The noise will scare away the wolves."

He paused to look around him, still gripping Beth tight to him. "Wolves? There's wolves around here?"

"Yes, I've seen them." Okay, it was only one, Wōden, the white one that followed the sheriff's sister-in-law Chloe everywhere. All the locals knew he wouldn't harm them, unless of course they threatened her or her little baby. "The jingle bells will keep them away." She had no idea if that was true, but this guy didn't either. He seemed as dumb as some of the kids in her school. Not smart like a grown up man should.

"Okay. Bring them, now come on." He marched Beth towards the trees, not waiting for her to catch up.

Callie hurried through the snow, stopping just before the trees to pull one of the sleighbells off and drop in in the snow. One of her favorite fairy tales was *Hansel & Gretel*. They used breadcrumbs to mark their path into the woods. She'd use the bells. Hopefully her dad would see them and know it was her.

Please, God, let Daddy find them.

*
**

Noel jogged to his truck parked on the far side of the town square. Gage wanted everyone to wait and get organized.

The hell with that. He wasn't waiting. That was his daughter out there. She was alone in the cold with a crazed kidnapper. Worse, she wasn't the one he'd meant to take. No, it had been the banker's daughter. Callie was extra baggage. Not important to the bastard who'd taken them, but she was his whole world.

He climbed in the driver's side and started the engine.

The passenger door opened and Monty jumped inside.

"You should stay here with Bruce," he said, gripping the steering wheel with both hands.

"He's in good hands with Dr. Roberts. Give me your cell phone," she said holding out her hand.

He didn't argue with her, but handed it over. Putting the truck in gear, he pulled out onto the snow-covered street. "This snow is getting worse."

"It's why the sheriff was asking for anyone with snowmobiles to get them." She plugged the phone into the charger and set it in the holder. "We want anyone who finds the girls to be able to call us. Mine is already charged. Also, do you have GPS tracking app for her phone?"

"Yes. If she has her phone with her and it's charged." He turned the corner of the town square and headed up the road the sleigh and the girls disappeared down. "Why didn't I remind her to do both?"

"Because you didn't expect something horrible like this to happen," she said, clutching the handrail in the passenger door as they slid on the slick road when he tried to stop at the crossroads.

With expertise, Noel turned into the slide and brought the truck back into control and a stop. "Roll your window down and see if you see the sleigh tracks on your side."

She did as he asked, holding her phone's flashlight to the right. "Nothing here."

"Nothing to the left either. I think the snow is filling in the tracks already." His voice shook—with rage or fear, she wasn't sure which.

He reached over and unlocked his phone, then hit the GPS app on his phone. Callie's phone came up with a green dot.

"Thank God it's on," he murmured.

Turning right, he hit his bright lights, to help them see up the road through the snow falling for anything moving and particularly the sleigh. As they turned, Monty saw a second set of car lights approaching the same stop sign. The lights on top of the SUV showed it was one of the sheriff's vehicles.

"People are following us."

Noel simply nodded, completely focused on maneuvering the road in front of them and heading in the direction the GPS said. Monty kept scanning the window in front of them and to the right side in case something was there, praying all the while they'd find both of the girls she'd come to care for in the short time she'd known them, and her beloved Sugarplum.

Suddenly, Noel hit the brakes and the tail end of the truck fishtailed. Once again, he managed to maneuver the car to gain control of it.

"What happened?" Monty asked gripping the handrail tight.

"The GPS isn't on the road anymore."

"He must've let Sugarplum go across the field."

A knock sounded on the driver's window. Monty jumped. Noel rolled his window down to find Deputy Daniel Löwe and Brody standing there.

"What's going on?" the deputy asked.

"We were following Callie's GPS," Noel answered.

Daniel nodded. "Good idea. Why'd you stop?"

"The bastard went off the road that direction," Noel said pointing out the window in a northeasterly direction. "We're going to have to go on foot."

"Okay." The deputy pulled out a SAT phone and dialed a number. "We've tracked them three miles east on Cooper. They've gone off the road. We'll be on foot," he said stepping away from the door as Noel raised the window.

Grabbing his phone, Noel turned to Monty. "You can drive back to town."

"That's the second time you've told me that," she said

putting on her gloves, then pulling her zipper to the top. "I'm going with you."

"I'm going to move fast." He didn't wait for her answer but climbed out of the truck and slammed the door.

She climbed out her side, slamming the door just as hard. "Didn't ask you to. I'll keep up. Thanks for coming, Brody," she said, nodding at the other man.

He didn't answer, but followed behind Noel.

Daniel fell into step with them as they crossed over onto the snow-covered field, still talking on the phone. "Gotcha, tell her we're heading northeast, towards the mayor's Christmas tree farm." He disconnected and put the phone in his pocket, pulling out his military grade flashlight. "Gage had Harriett and Wes go get their snowmobiles. They'll head this way."

"I'm not waiting," Noel threw over his shoulder. Callie was out there, and he needed to find her. He couldn't lose her too.

Chapter Twenty-Three

"Gage, I think there's someone we need to talk to," Bobby said, standing in front of him inside the civic center where all the people had gathered out of the snowstorm. He'd just hung up from relaying Daniel's message to Wes. He and Chloe had taken their two children to her cabin for the night to free up Bobby to help with the rescue mission.

"Who?" As always, when she talked with her husband, whether it was family or police business, she had his full attention.

"Try not to scare him off, but you see that young man standing in the corner? Jeans, black hoodie, sandy blond hair?"

Without moving his face even a fraction of an inch, her husband shifted his gaze slightly. "Nervous shift in his stance?"

"Yes. He was with another young man this afternoon in the marketplace eating. They looked like they might be brothers."

"And you think he might be our kidnapper?" Gage smiled as if she'd said something amusing, still not taking his gaze from the younger man.

"I do."

"Well, I've learned to trust your gut feelings over the years, my love. Why don't we both circle around to talk to him. You want to go left or right?"

She smiled up at him. "I'll go right. Want me to distract him?"

"You read my mind."

Stopping by the make-shift coffee table Lorna had assembled, she grabbed two cups of coffee, putting sugar in both, then headed towards the nervous young man, pasting on a concerned, yet friendly face so as not to make him bolt.

"Hope you don't mind, but you look like you could use a coffee," she said as she neared him.

"Uh, yeah. Thanks," he said turning his attention to her to take the coffee.

Out of her periphery Bobby saw Gage moving from one group of people to another, slowly making his way around behind the stranger.

"It's awful nice of you to come help with the search. Do you know the girls? Mr...?" she asked just as he was taking a sip of the hot liquid, keeping her voice calm and positive, a trick she'd learned over the years when she was a teacher.

He swallowed. "Barker. Kurt Barker. No, I don't know either of the girls. Have they got an idea where they went?"

Bobby shook her head. "No. And that's what has everyone worried. They're out there in the dark night, with more snow coming in and the temperature falling. We're afraid they could freeze to death."

His eyes went wide, his hand holding the cup of coffee shook slightly. "How long can they be out in the cold before that happens?"

"Depends on if they find any shelter," Gage said coming in behind him and startling the young man who instinctively moved closer to Bobby and stared up at her six-foot-four husband. "If they had somewhere to stay out of the cold, they might all live until morning."

Kurt's head was on a swivel as he looked from Gage to Bobby and back again. "You have to save them."

"We're doing our best to find them," Gage said, staring straight at Kurt. "If someone knew something that would help us, well we might find them faster."

"What are you going to do..." Kurt paused and swallowed nervously. "What are you going to do with him?"

"Well, now, that depends. If we find them and no one's hurt?" Gage shrugged. "Probably go a lot easier on him. Where did he take them?"

Bobby knew that look on Gage's face. Her husband was done playing nice cop. He wanted answers. Hopefully, Kurt would give them without anymore prodding or Gage might shake them out of him.

"He went the wrong way." Tears filled Kurt's eyes and he swallowed hard trying not to give into his emotions. Bobby had seen this on more than one teen over the years. "He doesn't know where he's going. It was the horse and sleigh. I knew I shouldn't have left him alone there."

"What's your brother's name? He is your brother, right?" Bobby asked as patiently as she could.

Kurt nodded. "Karl. He's slow, you know?"

"Is he going to hurt the girls?" Bobby asked.

Kurt shook his head. "No. He's just a big kid. He won't hurt them." He turned pleading eyes back up at Gage. "I swear he won't. Especially if I tell him not to, I'm supposed to look after him, but I don't know where they went."

"We've got the general direction. You come with me, and we'll go see if we can find them before it's too late." Gage laid his hand on Kurt's shoulder. "Don't give me any problem out there. Your brother's life, as well as those girls' lives, depends on us working together. Got that?"

Kurt nodded and the pair headed towards the door.

"Bobby, keep your radio close," Gage said over his shoulder. "And make sure your sister has the trauma unit ready. I don't know what we're bringing her."

Chapter Twenty-Four

"It's getting colder," Callie said as she tromped along behind the guy and Beth, dodging low hanging branches of evergreens and other kinds of trees as they wove their path in between them. As far as she could tell, the guy had no idea where he was going. She was tired of calling him *the guy*. "What's your name?"

"Karl," he muttered, dragging Beth over a fallen tree, both of them slipping before he caught his balance.

"OW! You're hurting me!" Beth complained.

Callie climbed over the tree and carefully landed beside them. "It's still getting colder. Is your hideout close?"

Her question made him stop moving and look around. She'd seen a deer one night standing in the middle of the road as her Uncle Nick drove her home from a volleyball meet. He'd stopped the truck before the deer was injured, but the headlights seemed to have hypnotized the animal. It just stared at them as if wondering what was happening. Karl had that same wide-eyed confused look.

He searched frantically for direction and tears filled his

eyes. For a moment, he reminded her of her little cousin Gabe when something was wrong and he was scared.

"If you're ever in a situation where you feel threatened. Keep your heart rate steady. Don't panic. You never know when an opportunity to turn the situation in your favor will happen."

Dad told her that after one of his overseas missions that he never talked about. He'd been having one of his life-lessons lectures about growing up and being in crowds of people when away from home. She hated listening to them, but they seemed to give him some comfort, so she did. Who knew they'd come in handy now? Her captor was as scared about being out in the dark forest as much as she and Beth.

Could she use this to her advantage?

"We need to find some shelter. The wolves like to come out in the cold," she said and jingled the bells still on the strip of cloth. She'd dropped some along their way, but gave up the idea when she realized he was moving in circles.

"I don't know," he said, grabbing Beth and moving her again. "I don't know."

"You have to remember," Callie said just as he neared a big evergreen with really low branches.

"Stop saying that!" he yelled, looking back at her. Then suddenly his feet went out from under him and he slammed into another over turned tree. His hold on Beth loosened and she fell the other direction.

"Oww!" he howled, grabbing his ankle.

In his fall, the gun flew out of his hand and was laying in the snow out of his reach.

Callie hurried forward and grabbed it, then got between him and Beth.

Noel stomped through the snow trying to follow the direction of Callie's GPS and the occasional lines of the sleigh's running blades that the wind was covering more and more. Desperation and fear willed him to keep moving. Often on his missions he'd been involved in rescue missions, but never one as important as this one.

He held the phone up and checked the direction. Still northeast towards the mayor's property. If they made it there, there were plenty of places for them to take shelter.

"Are we closer?" Monty asked just behind his left shoulder. The woman hadn't complained at the pace he was setting despite the uneven land they trampled across and the three or four inches of snow making their trek more difficult.

"They haven't moved far from the same point, but still on the same course."

"That's good isn't it?" she asked.

"I don't know. Maybe the horse got tired." He stopped. The snow had stopped, but the wind still whipped the fallen snow over the sled tracks. His heart sank. "Maybe one of them is injured. And at the pace we're slogging through this mess, if we do catch up with them, it might be too late."

"You can't think like that," Monty said, putting her hand on his arm. "You have to have faith that we'll find them."

"Faith in what? God?" He scoffed. "I prayed endlessly that he'd save Rebecca. That he wouldn't take her away from me and Callie. Then I switched to him relieving her pain on those nights when I'd hold her as she'd moan. He never answered those prayers."

"It's Christmas. A time to believe in miracles."

"I haven't prayed for that since Rebecca died. I don't think I can."

"I'll do it. You just listen," she said and took his hand.

Another hand landed on his shoulder. Brody had stopped

beside him. Daniel stood on his other side as Monty lifted a prayer for guidance and speed in finding the girls and bringing them home safely.

As if on cue, the sound of engines filled the night. Lights from three snowmobile headlights flashed in the dark as they drew near.

Harriett, Nick and deputy Wes Strong came to a stop. Behind Wes' snowmobile was a trailer sled with another snowmobile strapped on.

"We double up," Harriett said. "Brody, you're with me. Monty you stay with Noel. Dan, you're with Nick. That should distribute the body weight evenly. Noel, you lead since you have the GPS."

Noel and Daniel unloaded the extra vehicle while Harriett deftly removed the sled from the back of hers.

"I'll pick this up on the way back," she said.

Once they were all loaded, Monty held the GPS tracker up and Noel started out. She held on tight to him as they powered their way over the snow-covered terrain. They were making good distance then suddenly, Monty was pounding on his shoulder.

He stopped to find out her problem. The look of sadness and fear on her face told him it wasn't good.

"The GPS is gone."

Chapter Twenty-Five

Callie looked at the gun in her hand. It wasn't real.

"It's a toy! You scared us with a toy gun!" she yelled, getting in Karl's face where he sat huddled on the ground holding his leg.

"I'm sorry. I wanted her to come with me," he said, nodding at Beth, who stood quietly beside Callie. "Kurt says toy guns scare people as much as real ones, and no one really gets hurt."

"Well, they do. We're lost out here in the cold, dark night, because you scared us. If I knew this was a toy, I would've called my dad to come get us and stayed with Sugarplum." she pulled her phone out of her pocket. "And my phone is dead. Great! Just great!"

She pocketed it again, despite the fact she wanted to throw it at Karl's head.

"Callie?" Beth's quiet voice broke through the anger. "Is Sugarplum okay?"

Callie turned and wrapped her arm around her friend. "I'm sure she is. Remember Monty telling us how horses are better than people at handling the cold and the snow?"

"That's why they put on thicker coats in the winter," Beth said, sounding less worried.

"Horses don't wear coats," Karl muttered.

Callie scowled his direction. "Shows what you know. Horse's hair is called a coat and in winter it grows in thicker to protect them from the cold and wind."

"Wish we had a horse's coat," he muttered again, sounding even more dejected. "Kurt is gonna be so mad at me."

Callie continued to hug Beth close. It felt a little warmer that way. Maybe if they all three huddled together they'd all be warmer. Not that she really felt like hugging Karl, but she figured he might as well be good for something like keeping them all warm until her dad found them—and she had no doubt he would. Beside it was Karl's fault they were in this mess. She pulled Beth over near him, sat down beside him and pulled Beth down by her too. "Who's Kurt?"

"My brother. He was supposed to be with me. He's gonna be mad that I took her without him."

"That's like the tenth time you said you were supposed to take Beth. Why were you kidnapping her?"

"We weren't kidnapping her—"

"Yes, you were. Taking someone against their will, that's kidnapping," Callie corrected him.

He slumped, then gasped and grabbed his lower leg again. "We was just going to borrow her for a night, until her dad gave us some money from his bank. It was better than robbing another one."

Callie stared at him. "You rob banks?"

"Just little ones and only a few times. We ain't like Jesse James, although he had his brother with him too. I read it in a book once."

A gust of wind blew through pushing snow up around them.

All three of them shuddered and snuggled in closer. If they could find a place to keep the wind off them, it would help them stay warm. At least she thought so. Another gust shot through the tiny little clearing where they sat.

She closed her eyes and prayed inside her head just like her mom told her to do when she was little. *Please God, help us find a little bit of shelter.* Then she opened her eyes to scan their surroundings. It was so dark.

Suddenly, there was more light around them. She looked up through the tree branches. The clouds had parted and a star shone down almost like a spot light on a big evergreen whose lower limbs looked like a tent her Uncle Nick and Aunt Holly used to go camping.

"Hey, do you think you can walk?" she asked Karl.

"My leg hurts awful bad."

She wanted to say good and that he deserved it, but that wasn't going to help anyone right now. "I'm not asking you to walk a mile, just over to that big tree," she said pointing to where the starlight shone on the tree. "I think if we all fit under those branches, it might keep the wind off us at least for awhile."

He looked at the tree and then seemed to consider the pain he'd feel versus freezing out there by himself. "Yeah, I can make it. Might have to crawl though."

"Okay, Beth and I are going to go there. You follow and I'll hold the branches back for you to get in. Okay?"

He nodded. She got Beth to go with her and settled her in the middle of the nearly dry area beneath the evergreen boughs.

"Beth, I'm going to have Karl sit on one side of you and I'll be on the other."

"I don't like him," she muttered shaking her head at the idea.

"I don't really either, although he's a lot less frightening now

180

that he's hurt. But I got really warm when I was in the middle. I think you should get warm too. Okay?"

She made that funny little face she did when she didn't want to help scoop up horse poop in the stalls, but would do it anyway. Callie smiled. If she was able to make that face, her friend wasn't quite as scared as she had been.

Callie held the branches back just like she promised until Karl got there and scooted in on the outside of the little area. Before she got in her place, she looked back across the snow in the clearing. A dark trail of dots followed where Karl had hobbled. He must've cut something on his leg, because that was blood.

Another gust of wind came through and she hurried into the little make-shift shelter, letting the branches drop. It definitely helped with the wind.

"That's better, isn't it?" she said, trying to sound cheery for her two companions. Aunt Holly always said it's just as easy to be positive as negative.

"I'm still scared," Beth said.

Pulling out the sleigh bell collar that still had some of the bells attached, she gave it to Beth. "How about you jangle these some and maybe it will bring us some help.

"Like Santa?" Beth asked.

Callie smiled. "Sure."

She didn't believe in Santa. She never had. Her mother told her the gifts were from her and her dad. But tonight, she'd even take help from a big man in a red suit—Cleetus or Santa. But mostly, she was hoping to let her dad know where to find them. As Beth jangled the bells, Callie closed her eyes and prayed again that her dad would come soon.

"Kurt, why did your brother take those girls?" Gage asked as he turned onto Cooper Road and headed east, in the direction Daniel had relayed earlier.

Out of the corner of his eyes, Gage saw Kurt stiffen and he also went very silent. He hoped the kid wasn't going to force him to beat the information out of him, although he really only wanted confirmation on what he already suspected.

"You need to talk to me, Kurt. What were you planning to do with Beth when you kidnapped her?"

"We weren't going to hurt her. I swear it."

"What were you going to do?" Gage kept his voice even keeled as he maneuvered his truck down the center of the road. The wind gusts swirled the snow like mini tornadoes and made visibility hard.

"We were just going to keep her in an old shack I found in the woods beyond that horse farm."

"The Gentle Creek Ranch?"

Kurt shrugged. "Yeah, I guess that's the one. Anyways, we were just going to get her dad to give us some of that money I heard the state sends your town. Then we'd leave town with directions on where to find her. That's all."

"You know that's kidnapping and extortion. Both felonies."

Kurt slumped against the passenger door. "Yeah, but I couldn't risk robbing another bank."

"You two have been the ones robbing banks the last month or so, aren't you?" Again, Gage kept his questions more of a conversation than an interrogation. A confession wasn't going to hold up in court, since he hadn't read the guy his rights, but he wanted information right now. He'd decide what to do with it later.

"Yeah, we might've been there."

"Why'd you change your plan from bank robbery?"

"Karl. He almost got us caught. I was afraid he'd get shot or get me shot or make someone else get shot, so I thought we'd get the bank manager to bring us the money."

Gage slowed the truck for a turn in the road nearing the three-mile marker Daniel said they'd stopped at and gone by foot. "Is your brother armed?"

"No. Not with a real gun."

"What do you mean not a real gun?" Gage said, glancing his way then back to the road, the snow had stopped falling.

"Like I told you, my brother is slow. Like a little kid some-times. My mom was addicted to Meth by the time he was born. So, I would never keep a real weapon near him. He could hurt himself as much as anyone else. But if you wave a fake gun in people's faces, they really don't know the difference. So, we only carry toy guns."

Gage relaxed a little. At least the guy's little brother wasn't going to shoot the girls.

Up ahead he found both Noel's truck and the sheriff's SUV that Daniel was driving pulled off on the side of the road. He slowed as he pulled in behind them. Then he reached into the side panel of his truck, pulling out a pair of hand cuffs he kept there out of the reach of his son, and convenient if he needed them for a suspect, like tonight.

"You know I'm going to have to arrest you and your brother, right?" He held up the handcuffs and prayed the kid didn't decide to make a break for it. Chasing him down in the snow and cold would suck.

Kurt nodded and held out his hands. "I know. Can Karl and I be in the same cell? He's not used to being without me."

"I can't make any promises where you'll end up. But I think we can put you in the same cell in our jail." He put the cuffs on him, making sure they weren't too tight. Least he could do, since

183

he hadn't given him any grief about it. "Of course that's going to depend on whether or not those girls are found safe and sound."

*
**

Since the GPS went down, the rescue group elected to travel in the last known direction, albeit slower. As she rode along behind Noel through the dark night, Monty kept one arm wound tightly around his waist, clutching his coat in front. Using her own phone's flashlight feature, she scanned the tree line to their right, looking for any sign of Sugarplum, the red sleigh or the girls. The clouds started to thin. The snow had stopped, but the wind was now bitter cold.

She dreaded the thought of them all being out in this all night.

Suddenly, something popped up in the tree line.

She leaned in close to Noel's ear. "Stop!" she yelled over the roar of the snowmobiles' engines.

Immediately he stopped and looked in the direction she was pointing her flashlight light.

There, just outside the tree line of the forested area sat one giant red sleigh. Everyone else must've seen it too, because all four vehicles turned and made a beeline for the trees.

Please God let them be there. Please let them be alive. Please let them be unhurt.

As they neared, the sleigh moved. Sugarplum was still attached. The roar of the engines must be scaring her. Monty tapped hard on Noel's shoulder, then leaned in again. "Slow down. We don't want her to bolt."

He slowed and signaled the others to do the same. Monty didn't wait, but jumped off the snowmobile and ran as best she could through the snow drifts to her horse.

"It's me girl. You're alright," she said in her most soothing voice, loud enough for the mare to recognize her. It seemed to do the trick. Sugarplum stopped trying to pull the sleigh into the forest and turned her head towards Monty.

"Good girl." Monty kept talking soothingly until she was standing next to her horse and running her hands over Sugarplums neck.

"They're not here!" Noel said, slamming his fist on the back of the sleigh, then he began walking around the sleigh. "Did we miss them?"

"Stop moving," Harriett ordered.

"Why?" he asked, even though he did exactly what she said.

"Brody needs to see the ground for any tracks," she said, shining a high intensity light at the ground between. "Get started."

Brody stood his ground a moment. "I stopped taking orders when I left the military."

"Two girls are depending on you," Harriett said, this time her voice softening. "They need your help and your skills."

"Can you find them?" Noel asked, stepping closer.

Brody stared into his eyes. "I'll try."

Noel nodded and took a step back. "You lead. I'll follow."

"All three of them got out here," Brody said studying the ground on the right side of the sleigh. "Looks like the guy dragged the smaller girl."

"Beth," Monty said.

"Yeah," Brody acknowledged. "Callie followed."

"Just like we thought. She's trying to protect Beth," Noel said, following Brody as he walked past Monty and the horse.

"Looks like Sugarplum was trying to follow them, but couldn't get past the trees with the sleigh attached. Brody absently patted the horse as he moved past her, Noel and Nick on his heels.

Harriett grabbed the two backpacks strapped to the back of Wes' snowmobile, handing one to Monty. "Let's go."

Monty was torn, she wanted to help find the girls, but Sugarplum needed her reassurance.

Harriett gave her a little push. "Beth knows you, not the rest of us, really. Daniel can stay with the horse. Besides we'll need it to get the kids back to the trucks. Now come on."

Hefting her backpack onto one shoulder, Monty stepped in beside Harriett as they followed them into the woods. Wes, who was carrying a rifle, brought up the rear.

A few feet into the trees, Brody held up a fist and everyone stopped as he bent down to retrieve something. He gave it to Noel, then kept going.

Noel passed it to his brother who handed it to Monty.

A sleigh bell.

Callie must've dropped it and taken them with her to mark their trail. Smart girl. Monty pocketed it and kept moving, the sound of branches snapping beneath their feet the only sound.

"What special skills does Brody have?" she quietly asked Harriett after a while.

"He's former Airforce pararescue."

Well, that didn't tell her much. "And that means what?" she asked dodging an evergreen branch near her face. She was at least half a foot taller than the tiny older woman, who just ducked under the same branches.

"He was trained to parachute in behind enemy lines to find downed pilots no matter what terrain," Wes answered her. "He's a trained tracker and a paramedic."

"Oh." That made sense. It also explained why he was probably suffering from PTSD.

They hiked further into the forest, finding a sleigh bell every time the trail changed course. Monty wasn't a trained tracker like Brody or even an experienced hiker, but after a while, she

186

was pretty sure they were wandering around like a drunken pirate rather than trail blazing like Daniel Boone.

They traveled on. No more sleigh bells were found after the first six. Monty tried not to get discouraged. She knew there were probably ten more. Had the girls' captor realized what Callie was doing? Had he taken the bells away from her? Or had he hurt her and she could no longer leave the marked trail?

Chapter Twenty-Six

W as it his imagination or was there suddenly more light coming into the forest?

Noel looked up through the tree branches and saw the clouds thinning. Star light shown down on them. Up ahead was a small clearing.

Brody held his fist up and everyone froze. He shone his flashlight on the area and Noel's heart caught in his throat.

Blood. A small pool of it.

Was it Callie's? *Please God, don't let it be hers.*

As they stood quiet, a distinct sound rang out.

Jingle-jingle-jingle.

"Sugarplum's sleigh bells!" Monty whispered excitedly.

Wes moved around them just as Brody pulled a weapon from his coat pocket. He stepped forward and Wes moved into flank him. Noel and Nick went next.

Monty started to follow, only to have Harriett's hand land on her arm.

"We wait here. Just in case."

Noel glanced back and gave Monty a nod. She returned it showing she understood. Finding his daughter was the most important thing right now. He couldn't focus on that if he was worrying about Monty getting shot by some crazed kidnapper.

Brody motioned for them to spread out. Wes went left, Nick went right. Noel stayed with Brody as they followed the trail of blood towards a giant evergreen tree. He fought to keep his heart rate steady, not give into the fear coursing through him and he found himself praying.

Please God, don't let her be hurt. Don't let it be Callie's blood.

Jingling sounded again.

Brody pointed to the base of the tree where branches hung low like a canopy. He motioned that he'd go first on three. He handed Noel his flashlight then pointed to his own eyes. Noel nodded he understood. He'd use the light to distract or even blind the guy holding his daughter, so Brody could disarm him. Brody motioned to Nick to grab the branch. He moved forward, but stayed to the left of the tree.

Brody held up his fingers one at a time to the count of three.

Nick grabbed the thick branch and pulled it back.

Noel flashed the light inside.

Brody and Wes filled the space between Noel and the three frightened faces silhouetted in the beam of light.

All three people in the little grotto made from the tree trunk and low evergreen branches screamed.

"Hands up! Sheriff's department!"

The guy sitting nearest the exit held up his hands.

"Daddy!" Callie yelled, scrambled from her spot and threw herself at Noel.

He caught her just like he did when she was a tiny little girl and hugged her tight, tears streaming down his cheeks. Someone nudged him and he moved to the side to let Monty in.

"Beth?" she said holding out her arms.

"Monty!" Beth hurled herself at her.

Noel moved back, keeping his arm around his daughter. "Are you alright? Are you hurt?"

"No, Daddy. I'm okay, just cold."

Monty brought Beth out and asked her the same questions. Beth just shook her head no.

"Get up," Wes said pointing his weapon at the kidnapper.

"I can't."

Wes reached in and grabbed his arm to haul him to his feet.

"Ahh," the kid screamed.

Callie tried to pull free. "Don't hurt him!"

Noel held her fast. "Stay back, Callie."

"Daddy, he's hurt. He fell and is bleeding from his leg."

"It's okay, sweetie. Brody's a medic and Miss Harriett's here. They'll take a look at him, but we've got to get you all back to the sleigh and to the cars, first."

"Do you have a weapon?" Wes asked as he frisked him, his rifle slung back over his shoulder by the strap.

"No," the guy said a bit dejectedly.

Callie and Beth giggled.

"What's so funny?" Monty asked.

Callie reached in her coat pocket and pulled out what looked like a gun. "He dropped this when he fell. It's a toy. Not real."

"But he did scare us with it," Beth said. She turned to the guy as Brody helped him hobble out from beneath the tree. "That wasn't very nice of you."

Their kidnapper shrugged, looking more like a sullen teen than a menace. "I'm sorry."

"Chat later," Harriett ordered. "Let's get them out of this cold before we all have hypothermia. Nick, you help Brody get this young man back to the sleigh."

"Gladly. I'll walk him all the way to jail, if I have to," his brother said, coming up to grab hold of the injured boy's arm.

"You're lucky you didn't hurt my niece, or I'd be beating you to a pulp."

"Don't threaten him. He's the patient."

Nick met Noel's gaze. If the kid tried anything, neither of them could promise he would arrive at the sleigh in the same condition he was in now.

"He isn't going to try to run. He probably has a broken ankle," Harriett said. She turned on her heels and started back the way they'd come with everyone following.

Noel kept his arm around Callie the entire way, as if he was afraid if he left go, she'd disappear. In front of them, Monty did the same with Beth as they navigated their way through the forest.

"I'm sorry I got in the sleigh, Daddy," Callie said quietly. "But I couldn't let Beth get in there alone, especially when Karl snapped the reins and Sugarplum bolted. I didn't know what else to do."

Pride in her replaced some of the fear still lingering in him. He hugged her tighter. "You did the right thing. You left us the sleigh bells to follow, didn't you?"

She grinned up at him, then took his hand to climb over a fallen tree. "I thought you'd see it and find me."

"How could I not. You made me read you *Hansel & Gretel* so many times I knew it by heart, especially the part where they left a trail of breadcrumbs."

They broke through the tree line at the exact spot where Daniel stood stroking Sugarplum' neck.

"Got your SAT phone?" Harriett asked him.

"Hello, to you too," Daniel said, pulling the phone out of his coat pocket. "Everyone okay?"

Harriett took a thermos out of her backpack. "Get Gage on the phone. Tell him all three are recovered. One injured. Will

191

need transport to the hospital." She turned to Monty. "You drive this thing?"

"I can handle it," she said, helping Beth up into the front seat. "Let me check out Sugarplum first."

Harriett poured what smelled like hot chocolate into a cup and handed it to Beth. "Careful. It's a little hot."

"Thank you, Miss Harriett," Beth said with a smile which Harriett returned. Then she pulled a second metal cup from her bag.

"Callie, you ride up here with Beth and Monty. Your dad can sit in back with our patient."

Callie didn't argue, just climbed up next to Beth and took the cup of hot chocolate the nurse offered her. Noel wanted to demand she stay with him, but he knew he was being ridiculous. She was safe. If he tried to smother her, even this close to her abduction, things might never feel normal for her or him. Instead, he found a blanket on the seat and spread it over the two girls to help them stay warm.

"Let's get you up in the seat, tough guy," he said instead, focusing on getting her abductor in the back of the sleigh.

"Ow," the kid moaned as he hit his foot on the side of the sleigh.

"Careful. We don't want you to get hurt anymore," Nick said, and Noel knew his brother wanted the exact opposite, as did he. A little extra pain for endangering Callie and Beth? Some for the fear he'd cause both their family and Beth's? Even a little more for the aggravation at having to hunt him down? Yeah, excuse him and his brother if their empathy level for this guy wasn't too high right now.

Once everyone was settled—the girls in front with Monty, Noel and Nick flanking Karl in back—Harriett and the deputies, along with Brody mounted on the snowmobiles and headed out. Monty gave them a head start so as not to rattle Sugarplum, then snapped the reins lightly to get them moving.

A welcoming party awaited them at the spot where they'd left the trucks. The sheriff and the county paramedics were there, along with Beth's parents. Brody and the paramedics stabilized Karl's foot and leg, which had some bone sticking out of it just above the ankle. It was determined he'd need transport to the hospital. Gage made everyone wait while he officially arrested Karl and his brother who already was in handcuffs before he could go to the hospital.

"I'll take you over to be with your brother," he told the one named Kurt, then put him back in his truck. "Daniel?"

"Yes, Sheriff?" his deputy asked.

"You relieve me at the hospital in an hour for the rest of your shift. I'll have Jason take over at the jail tonight."

"Yes, sir." Daniel turned to Brody. "Need a lift back to town?"

"Might as well," Brody answered, walking towards the sheriff department SUV.

"Brody," Noel called and jogged over to him. "Thanks for helping."

Brody gave him a shrug, but didn't break eye contact. "They're good kids. Wouldn't want them freezing out here." They shook hands, then Brody started for the SUV once more. He paused. "That job offer still open?"

"Yep," Noel said.

"I'll see you Monday then, oh, and tell Ms. Taylor I'd like to come see Percy some."

"Will do," Noel said as the man walked away.

Gage was talking to the girls when Noel came back. "Do you think you could come in tomorrow with your parents and tell me and Bobby all about what happened tonight?"

Callie exchanged a look with Beth, who nodded. "Yes, sir. We can. But he didn't hurt us. Only scared us some."

"We'll talk about it all tomorrow," he said with a tender look at the girls. "I think your parents very much want to get you both home." Then he looked at Monty standing by Sugarplum and the sleigh. "Bruce is at the Peaches 'N Cream waiting on you. Dylan stitched up his cut and did an MRI. No concussion, but said he might have a headache tonight."

"Thanks, I'll pick him up."

Gage extended his hand to Noel who took it. "Glad they're both home okay. I don't blame you for going after them without waiting. If it had been one of my kids, I'd have done the same thing."

"Glad you sent backup."

"Harriett?" Gage said with a slight shake of his head and climbed in his truck's driver side. "That woman does what she wants no matter who thinks they're in charge. I've learned to stay out of her way."

Everyone had left except Noel, Callie and Monty. He clicked the unlock button and the starter for his truck. "Get inside and get warm, Callie. I want to talk to Monty for a moment."

She ran over to her and gave her a hug. "Thanks for coming to find us."

Monty smoothed her hand over his daughter's face. "Sweetie, I'm so glad you and Beth are safe. I'm sorry the young man used your love of Sugarplum and the sleigh to scare you."

"I was more scared for Beth. And Sugarplum, because he didn't know anything about how to get her to slow down. I'm sorry I couldn't stop him from making her go so fast. I was afraid she'd get hurt or something."

"Oh, sweetie. You did nothing wrong. I'm glad you were there with them, even though your dad and I were worried about you." Monty hugged her again, looking over at Noel standing behind them. He read in her eyes the love she had for his daughter. She stepped back and smiled at Callie. "Now you go with your dad and I'll get Sugarplum and Bruce back to the farm. We can talk more tomorrow night at the dinner and you can tell me all about what happened. Okay?"

Noel waited until his daughter was in the truck, then turned to Monty. "Thanks for being there for her. And for praying with me. I...I," he choked on the words, all the adrenaline from the frantic fear he'd been under since he realized Callie was missing suddenly bursting out of him.

Monty stepped closer and wrapped her arms around him, holding him tight. "She's okay. Sometimes prayers are answered with a no. But sometimes, they're answered immediately and are blessings. Let's go with this one being a blessing."

"Always the optimist."

She leaned back to stare at him with a smile. "Better to believe in miracles than expect tragedy. And sometimes people are put in our lives at just the right time for a purpose. Like when you walked into my barn and realized how unsafe it was. I'll take that as a blessing."

"I will too." He lowered his head and tenderly kissed her. It had been years since he'd kissed a woman. He hadn't wanted to care about another woman after Rebecca's death because it hurt too much to lose them, but this woman had crept under that wall and made him want to kiss her, hold her, care about her.

Before he could let the kiss go deeper, he remembered his teenage daughter was in the truck and probably watching them. Slowly, he lifted his lips from hers. "I should get Callie home."

"I know. I have to go. Bruce gets cantankerous when he's up past his bedtime."

He chuckled. "You go first, and we'll follow you back to town."

Monty waved at Callie, understanding on her face. "I'll see you tomorrow?"

"Of course. I can't wait to try that brisket."

She laughed and climbed back on the sleigh. "You'll be impressed," she said snapping the reins.

He moved out of the way to watch her maneuver the horse and sleigh onto the road back to town, the taste of her still on his lips. "I already am."

Epilogue

A knock sounded on the door just after dark on Christmas Eve.

"Wonder who that can be?" Bruce asked.

They'd finished their dinner and were seated near the fireplace munching down on some popcorn while they played Texas hold'em poker. He'd taught her to play his favorite game when she'd first arrived at the ranch in Texas. They never bet with real money, often using peanuts or some other snack instead. Tonight, it was red and green candies.

"I don't know. I wasn't expecting anyone," Monty said as she went to answer it.

When she looked out the window, she saw Noel standing on the porch. Callie was out in the truck. She'd seen them almost every night since the botched kidnapping event.

The next morning, she'd met them at the sheriff's office. After Callie and Beth gave their statements to the sheriff, a meeting between herself, Noel and Beth's parents took place with the sheriff and Westen's district attorney, Kent Howard about the two Barker brothers. Gage had decided to hold Kurt in the cells at his office rather than the big jail below the courthouse. His younger brother had surgery earlier that morning for his compound fractured leg and the deputies were taking shifts sitting in his room. Gage took Kurt over to see him and having him in the office cells made that more convenient for his deputies.

"*These two boys are going to be charged with the local rash of bank robberies,*" Kent said. "*It's a federal crime and they'll serve time in a federal penitentiary for that.*"

"*What about kidnapping our kids?*" Jay Watters asked.

"*That's why I wanted you, your wife and Noel to come for this meeting,*" Gage said. "*We can charge Karl with the actual kidnapping and his brother for putting the idea in his head. It will hit the newsfeed and get spread over the state and possibly the whole country. The reason behind their attempt to hold Beth hostage was them wanting the money in your bank the state sends the town.*"

"*All of which is true,*" Jay said, looking confusingly at his wife.

"*That it is,*" Gage acknowledged. "*But the boy was technically unarmed, and although they were scared, neither of them were harmed. You might say, he got his own punishment with that broken leg. But letting the brothers' reason for this incident get national attention...*"

"*You're afraid it will put the idea in someone more lethal's mind,*" Noel said.

"*Exactly. We can hold them accountable with the bank robbery charges and keep Westen out of the limelight.*"

Jay and his wife exchanged looks.

"*Beth would be safer if we did that, wouldn't she?*" Vanessa asked.

"*I think we'll all be a little more cautious with her safety from now on,*" Gage said. "*But yes, I do think so.*"

"*Then we should do what you think would be best,*" she said.

Gage turned a questioning look to Noel.

"Callie is okay. In fact, she's been telling me how if it hadn't been for the toy gun, the sleigh ride was almost like a winter roller coaster ride. So, I'll be happy with just the bank robbery charges. They'll spend years in a federal penitentiary."

Gage nodded at Kent, who turned to Monty. "There's the matter of your horse, Ms. Taylor. Technically, he took her without your permission, so we can charge Karl with second degree theft with regards to your horse, since she's a therapy assistant animal."

Monty considered what he was asking. Did she want to add more jail time to the brothers? "You know what, Mr. Howard? Sugarplum was unharmed, as was the sleigh. It's Christmas time. I'd prefer not to press charges for that. If that's okay with you and not something required by law to pursue?"

"Then there's one more thing I'd like to explain to you," Gage said, picking up a pen and playing with it as he talked. "I've had some long talks with Kurt Barker. The kid has confessed to all the bank robberies, but just like yesterday, the only weapons they ever had were toy guns. He said he didn't want to risk his brother accidentally shooting someone. He's been responsible for his brother since even before their mother died of an overdose. Callie told us in her statement that Karl was like one of the boys in her class. Bobby talked with him this morning. She'd guess his mental age at about twelve, not his chronological age of nineteen."

"What are you saying?" Noel asked.

"Based on these circumstances, I think we should try to get these two a little bit of help," Gage said, looking them all straight in the eye, one at a time. "We know they're going to prison. But Karl isn't going to survive there on his own, not in a federal maximum facility. But in the spirit of Christmas, we'd like to talk with the feds, when they come to take custody of the pair and *recommend they serve time together and in a minimum security prison."*

They'd all agreed, and the feds were happy to have the bank robbers caught, promised to take under consideration everything the group talked about.

That night not only was her brisket a hit with everyone at the Yuletide Jubilee dinner, but she'd gotten to dance with Noel more than once. They'd sat with her at the church service the next day and he quietly teased her about mouthing the words to all the carol hymns the congregation sang. Later that week she and Callie laughed over their shared fiasco of an attempted gingerbread build, to which Noel suggested it was more of a gingerbread house in need of renovation. There'd been a snowball fight after Callie aome to help with the horses and an evening working Bruce's jigsaw puzzle while they had Callie's cookies and hot chocolate. Then there'd been the walks with Noel in the cold winter air and the kisses that grew more intimate each time they'd been alone.

This was turning out to be the best Christmas ever.

She opened the door. "Hi, what's up?"

"I need you to come with me. I need you to help me with something," he said, looking very serious.

"Is something wrong? Is Callie hurt?" she asked.

"No. She's fine. I just need to do something and I need your help to do it."

She reached for her coat. "Bruce, I'll be back," she yelled.

Noel took her hand and practically dragged her down the porch steps, as she was trying to button her coat. "You're sure nothing is wrong?"

"It will be if we don't get this done tonight," he said, opening the door so she could climb into the passenger side. Callie had climbed into the back seat.

"What's going on?" she asked the teen, who gave her a shrug.

"I don't know. He just said we needed to come get you."

The Trans-Siberean Orchestra played on the radio as they drove to town. Noel didn't say another word the entire trip and Monty grew worried.

"Are you at least going to tell me where we're going?" she asked as the neared the town square.

He pulled to a stop next to the Christmas tree. He climbed out and came around to her door and opened it. "I need you to come with me. Callie, you stay in the truck."

"Why?" his daughter asked, not quite reaching the whiney stage.

"This is something Monty and I need to do. Alone," was all he said.

Mont looked over her shoulder at Callie, who shrugged, looking confused. Apparently she was as much in the dark as she was about her father's problem.

He held his hand out to her. "Please? It's getting late."

"Okay." She put her hand in his and climbed out of the truck. He continued to hold it as they walked across the town square, past the Christmas tree to the gazebo.

Monty's heartbeat quickened, knowing what he had planned.

They went up the steps to stand just below the large ball of mistletoe covered in twinkling white fairy lights and red holiday ribbons.

"And why have your brought me here?" she asked, trying not to grin at him.

"Well. I've truly enjoyed getting to know you and spend time with you these past weeks. It's a little soon to be committing to anything more than continuing to explore this new relationship," he said.

"I agree. I've also enjoyed it, but it's a little fast for me too," she said, growing as serious as the look in his eyes.

"That being said, I don't always believe in traditions or curses, but," he looked up.

"You're afraid if we don't kiss under this, everything will eventually end in a not so good way," she finished for him.

"And since it's almost midnight on Christmas Eve—" he said, pulling her into his arms.

"We should commit to kissing beneath the Kissing Bough," she said smiling up at him. "Just in case."

He lowered his head to hers. "Just in case."

Callie looked at the clock on her phone and pumped her fist. Five minutes before midnight. They just made the cutoff. This was the best Christmas in a long, long time.

Newsletter sign-up

Thank you for reading
CLOSE TO SLEIGH BELLS
Want to know more about my books and new releases?
Please consider joining my **newsletter** mailing list.
I promise not to SPAM you.
Your email will NOT be sold to other sites
and is only to be used for the purpose of sending
out my newsletter.

Also by Suzanne Ferrell

About the Author

***USA Today bestselling author*, Suzanne Ferrell** discovered romance novels in her aunt's hidden stash one summer as a teenager. From that moment on she knew two things: she loved romance stories and someday she'd be writing her own. Her love for romances has only grown over the years. It took her a number of years and a secondary career as a nurse to finally start writing her own stories.

The author of 20 novels and an Amazon best-seller for both her series, the Edgars Family Novels and the Westen series, Suzanne's books have been finalists in the National Reader's Choice Awards--SEIZED (2013) and VANISHED (2014). Suzanne was also a double finalist in the Romance Writers of America's 2006 Golden Heart with her manuscripts, KIDNAPPED (Long Contemporary Category) and HUNTED (Romantic Suspense).

Currently working on more books for her Edgars Family series (KIDNAPPED, HUNTED, SEIZED, VANISHED, EXPOSED and Capitol Danger) and the Westen Series (Close To Home, Close To The Edge, Close To The Fire, Close To Christmas, Close To The Mistletoe, Close To Santa's Heart and Close To Danger), Suzanne hopes to bring readers more passionate and suspenseful books to fill your reading moments.

Suzanne's sexy stories, whether they are her on the edge of your seat romantic suspense or the heartwarming small town stories, will keep you thinking about her characters long after their Happy Ever After is achieved.

You can Find Suz at:

Website: <http://suzanneferrell.com/>